THE SAND CRABS

A Novel
by
M. E. Morris

Russell Dean & Company, Publishers
Santa Margarita, California

Other Books by M.E. Morris

Stealth
(Avon Books, 1996)

Biostrike
(Avon Books, 1996)

H. Norman Schwartzkopf:
Road to Triumph
(St. Martin's Press, 1991)

The Last Kamikaze
(Random House, 1990)

Sword of the Shaheen
(Presidio Press, 1989)

The Icemen
(Presidio Press, 1988)

The Alpha Bug
(Presidio Press, 1986)

THE SAND CRABS
by
M.E. Morris

First Printing : April, 1999

Published by Russell Dean & Company, Publishers, 22595 K Street, Santa Margarita, California, 93453-0349. All rights reserved. No portion of this book may be reproduced in any form without the express written consent of the publishers.

Library of Congress Cataloging-in-Publication Data.

Library of Congress Catalog Card Number: 99-60899

Morris, M.E.
The Sand Crabs / M.E. Morris p.cm.—
(Russell Dean fiction –novel)
1. Novel.   2. Fiji   I. Title.   II. Series. 1999-2000

ISBN 1-891954-30-X

Russell Dean books are printed on acid-free paper, and meet the guidelines for permanence and durability of the Committee on Production Guidelines for Book Longevity of the Council on Library Resources.

Printed in the United States of America.

DEDICATION

For the generations of
honorable men and women
who are now leaving for
a much better place.
Ours was a different time.

THE SAND CRABS

A Novel
by
M. E. Morris

April 30, 2000

Cindy —
Best wishes to a
fellow lover of the
written word.

M.E. Morris

Russell Dean & Company, Publishers
Santa Margarita, California

AUTHOR'S NOTE

This is a work of fiction but it is based on a life of fact. And in a certain sense, it is my epitaph.

I hope that it is premature.

I also intend that it be a tribute to a wartime acquaintance, Petty Officer Third Class Terumichi Nakai, Imperial Japanese Navy. We became friends.

This story is one of those that flow from the life experiences of the author.

Nevertheless, the events are fictional, as are all of the characters with the exception of the brief inclusion of Fijian General Sitiveni Rabuka in a fictional role.

Alas, Vaka Malua is also a figment of the author's imagination.

CHAPTER 1

THE ARRIVAL

Polynesian sunsets are like no others.

As the sun settles toward the western horizon, the brilliant blue of the Pacific sky seems to tire and begins a long night's sleep. At first, its fade is almost imperceptible as traces of orange and yellow are born and begin to bleed across the heavens. The colors deepen and there is a feeling that a wondrous thing is about to occur. And it does.

If there are clouds on the horizon, the fuzzy gray bottoms begin to brighten while the billowing tops fight to retain the brilliance of the last sunrays that now originate from well below the visible horizon. The towering cumuli are so temporarily successful in their capture of the last sunlight, they become iridescent. In a display of intense color the sky starts to glow and then surpasses its own brilliance with cloud-crowns of backlighted silver.

At that moment of transition, the reds appear and gently spread across the entire western sky. They absorb the yellows and oranges and mix with them into a horizontal blend of color that is neither red nor orange nor yellow yet is all three, so perfectly combined that they become a single swath of indescribable beauty. The dominant effect is an emerging deep red—a red that overwhelms as it reaches out. It seems to physically meld with your own being. You stand transfixed, overpowered by the beauty of nature.

The whitecaps pick up the red. In their lazy travel over one wave and up another they become a light pink. The sandy beaches glow with an identical tint and the sky reaches a peak of translucent color that even the most sophisticated cameras fail to capture.

The magnificence can only be truly seen by the human eye and in those brief moments when it is present, Man cannot help but gaze in awe at such spectacle. In all its splendor, it reflects the primal sides of Man, his adventurous side, his yearning to compete and surpass, his aggressive warrior nature and his willingness to die for what he believes. The Polynesian sunset is a glimpse of Valhalla.

Such was the sky as I lowered the mainsail of my 45-foot Boston-built sloop, the *Mary Margaret*. The broad-beamed white hull was slicing through southern Fijian waters and it rolled a bit more upright. Only the jib provided a few knots of forward speed across a calm sea in a light wind.

My name is Donald Foster. I am retired now after a very productive life in the business of international trade. For the last ten years the sea, particularly the South Pacific, has been my second home and it is the sea that gives me life and purpose. I relish the feeling of being so tiny amidst the vast waters and sky and my wonderment includes the stars that are always with me during the night. The moon is my guardian angel and when it wanes, my feeling of security does also. But both always return. This particular day had been unusually pleasant with steady following winds and a friendly sea.

I allowed the autopilot to continue steering. Just ahead, a thin irregular line lay across the darkening horizon. My favorite island, Vaka Malua, was a speck of sand-ringed tropical rain forest I purchased in 1994. I had renamed it, the English translation of the Fijian name being "slowly." And that was characteristic of my lifestyle whenever I was on the island.

It was too late in the day to move into the lagoon that surrounded the island. There was only one narrow entrance through the white coral reef that circled it and at ebb tide—which was now—the currents could be tricky. It took a bit of precise and steady seamanship to navigate through the narrow, curved passage and I liked that. Unwanted visitors would not bother me. But I was not anxious to tackle it in the darkness despite my confidence that I could do so if there were a strong need.

Instead, I would close a few miles and lay to during the remainder of the night, then at dawn power up the diesel to navigate through the passage and on to my anchorage.

Upon hearing the mainsail drop, feeling the heel lessen and the speed slow, Niko Timaru, one of the two Polynesian crewmen who regularly sailed with me, came up from below. He secured the canvas to the boom in neatly layered folds, wrapping each with bleached white tiedown lines.

"We'll anchor in the morning, Niko," I called out.

"Aye, captain. Sarah has dinner ready if you wish to go below."

Niko's wife was the other crewmember, as handy with canvas and coiled line as with spatula, natural herbs and fresh sea fish. Niko and Sarah, both in their late twenties, had been married for seven years and had sailed with me and my wife for the last five of those until the real-life Mary Margaret had died.

Mary Margaret had succumbed to the ugly spread of the berserk cellular beast that had first crept into her left breast almost twenty years in the past. Then, under vicious attack by teams of medicinal chemicals that were so cruel to my wife, even though their battle was on her behalf, the cancer had disappeared. Remission, the doctors had called it. But it was only sleeping.

A year later, rejuvenated and anxious to feed again on Mary Margaret's flesh, the evil thing reappeared and literally ate her alive as she refused the resumption of treatment, preferring to spend all except her last painful days at sea with me and the sky and the stars. It was a brave choice, and one for which she had paid dearly. In retrospect, I took quiet pride in her decision to die fighting rather than wallowing in self-pity. A renewed flood of chemicals would have beached her but not have improved her quality of life. She loved the sea as much as I, and now her ashes were part of the Pacific. In fact, they were part of the lagoon surrounding Vaka Malua.

This was my first visit since I had scattered them among the tropical flowers the Timarus and I had sprinkled on the surface of the water. As I spread the gray ash, a gentle handful at a time, Niko and Sarah sang a beautiful Hawaiian song that told of a pair of ancient young lovers, denied union by their parents, who had simply sailed out to sea in the boy's canoe and never returned. The flowers had long since disappeared but my beloved Mary Margaret would still be there. Tomorrow I would be with her.

"No, Niko," I responded, "I think I'll eat out here. Why don't you go below and enjoy a meal with Sarah. You can take the watch afterwards."

"Thank you, sir. It is a beautiful evening, one that Miss Mary would surely enjoy." I could see that Niko was not sure he should have made the last remark; it had been spontaneous but in his mind, perhaps not appropriate.

On the other hand, I appreciated it, for it demonstrated the closeness the four of us had shared. I tried to put him at ease. "She is doing that, enjoying this evening, just as we are. Tomorrow, we'll be with her, Niko."

"I'll be up soon, sir."

"Take your time. I'm not alone."

Sarah brought up my dinner.

❀   ❀   ❀

I awakened just before dawn. After I stretched some of the stiffness out of my bones, I slipped on shorts and worn gym shoes. In the small galley I found and opened a can of pear halves before I stepped up onto the cockpit deck of the *Mary Margaret*.

Sarah was on watch, minding the helm as the autopilot steered us toward Vaka Malua. The island was only a mile or so off our bow.

"Good morning, Sarah," I said. The predawn sunlight was rapidly covering the eastern sky and by the time I had finished my can of pears the white-hot silver rim of the sun was peeking above the horizon.

"Good morning, Captain," Sarah responded with a voice that was as sweet and mellow as the morning's breeze. She showed no signs of fatigue although she had probably relieved Niko about four. She stood erect on the left edge of the cockpit, her back braced by the port taffrail. Her eyes drank in the beauty of the lagoon beyond the reef. Her waist-long black hair responded to the caress of the mild Pacific wind and her dark skin glistened in the light oil that she used not to protect but to enhance it. She was the perennial Polynesian, the mysterious

5

beauty of the Pacific Triangle who had captured the white men's minds and imaginations since they had first ventured into the central Pacific, four hundred years after the ocean natives. I stood in quiet admiration only long enough to be rejuvenated by her natural beauty. I would not allow myself to invade her person by staring. Niko joined us.

"Secure the jib," I directed and Niko went forward to drop the small triangular sail. "I relieve you, Sarah," I added, starting the diesel.

"It is another God's day," Sarah commented. She smiled and breathed deeply of the sea air. "The island is beautiful. I will soon have a fresh flower for my hair."

Ahead, Vaka Malua, the green flora of its lush tropical rain forest dripping the moisture left over from the night's showers, lay under a stationary white cloud. A few budding ocean cumuli were beginning their daily buildup, white puffs of sky cotton that foretold another typical day. By afternoon, they would be massive creatures, some content to float with the sea wind, others angry and dumping their moisture in great sheets of water that would stir the surface of the ocean and thoroughly wet any mariner who sailed under them. If one had already reached such maturity, I would gladly have taken any reasonable detour to wash down the *Mary Margaret* and free her from the topside salt residue. But the newborn clouds were just in their infancy; they would wet themselves later on. Besides, the *Mary Margaret* was conditioned to wear a light crystal coating.

Later, after we had anchored, Niko would scrub down her teakwood decks and spend his first day at anchor cleaning the topside brass and making the minor repairs that were always necessary after a long voyage. We had left Honolulu fourteen

6

days back. Sarah would package whatever trash remained and tidy up the living quarters and galley.

The *Mary Margaret* carried two staterooms, a master and an ample double; fore and aft heads; a surprisingly roomy main salon with comfortable seating for six as well as an ingenious dining area that folded away when not in use. In a separate compartment set at the top of the ladder leading to the cockpit was the communications gear and accessible from the helm were the Global Positioning Satellite navigation system and the traditional binnacle.

A small, rectangular radar weather antennae rotated on the masthead, its main viewing scope in the cockpit and a small repeater in the aft cabin wall. There was also a search mode that would produce a reliable land return whenever anything was within its maximum range of seventy-five miles. At the moment, it was on the five-mile range and the green phosphorescent return clearly defined the reef and the south beach of Vaka Malua.

Eagerly, I manned the small rudder wheel on the starboard side of the forward cockpit bulkhead and adjusted the throttle to give the *Mary Margaret* a steady but safe five-knot speed through the winding opening in the reef. The sloop slid through and I fed in enough right rudder to steer toward the anchorage.

Good morning, Mary Margaret. I've missed you so.

For all of my love of sailing and relaxed retired life style, I was still a businessman. On my island I had built a compact village consisting of a central hut that housed a small stock of general store merchandise, and five individual guest *bures* that sat on stilts in the lagoon. They were accessible by short walk-ways from the beach, as were an open air dining room and lounge. I only rented to those whom I knew, those of my friends who could afford to exchange an arm and a leg for a few days in my remote Pacific paradise. For this period of my visit, all the *bures* were deliberately vacant.

I kept my staff year-round: manager, cook, maintenance man, barkeep, maid and dining area attendant. All but one were Polynesian, faithful employees I had brought out from Honolulu. The dining room attendant was Fijian. All six stood at the water's edge and waved as I steered the *Mary Margaret* toward her anchorage. It was not a difficult point to reach once you passed into the lagoon and there was enough depth and breadth to be casual about where you dropped anchor. I approached into the wind and throttled back to idle. When there was no relative motion over the water, I sang out, "Drop the hook, Niko! We're home."

Niko released the forward anchor and watched the chain play out. I let the sloop drift downwind until the steel flukes gained a solid purchase on the bottom. Then, I shut down the engine. "Secure the bow," I ordered.

Niko double-checked the set, fastened a steel keel line to the anchor chain so the strong keel rather than the anchor windlass would handle the stress. It was a special rig I had designed. Moving around on the bow, he made sure any extra lines were neatly coiled and out of the way.

I raised my arms over my head and waved back at the peo-ple on shore. Enthusiastically, I clapped my hands in a gesture of appreciation for their work during my absence. I knew them well and they were a loyal and hard-working group. Those who rented the few *bures* paid big bucks, but part of their pleasure was the service and pampering they enjoyed from my staff.

Niko was rigging the Zodiac over the side.

"Take Sarah and the trash ashore," I called out, "I'm going to stay out here a few minutes. Pick me up in, say, half an hour. Wait! Belay that, I'll swim in." It was barely fifty yards to the beach.

"Will do, Skipper," Niko replied. I grinned to myself. At sea, I was "Captain." Once we headed for the beach I was the more casual "Skipper." It was a subtle difference that marked the passage of our relationship from the strict regime of sailing the open ocean to the fun side of a port call. I was fortunate to have two such people who were both my crew and my friends.

Sarah and her trash bags dropped into the Zodiac and she cast the rubber boat off for the beach. Childlike, she waved at me. I waved back at her and Niko.

I made a casual walkaround inspection of the weather deck, double-checking the anchor rigging and making sure that the cockpit was secured before sitting on the bow, legs dangling over the side.

We're alone now, Mary Margaret. I love you so.

Here the water was as clear as the air. I could see the bottom of the lagoon alive with fish. Their kaleidoscope of colors sparkled with reflected sunlight. A black ray, its long barbed tail waving in its own wake, cruised the bottom while several large fish, probably groupers, swam with their wide mouths partially open, searching for meal opportunities. The food chain was alive and well.

Memories flooded my mind, one on top of another with such rapidity that I had to mentally work to slow down the torrent of past images.

Mary Margaret and I had found this to be our favorite place. Our annual two-week sail from Honolulu to Vaka Malua provided us the privacy and companionship we were never able to achieve on shore. It was regrettable that such satisfaction had come so late in life. I was a year older than Mary Margaret, who had died at 69.

Sure, Niko and Sarah were on board but discreetly kept to themselves when they were not on watch. The four of us were unavoidably together during the day but at night, the devoted Polynesians would generally stay below, policing the salon and performing the many small tasks that were always in need of being done. By ten in the evening, they were in their forward cabin, for it was customary for them to stand the mid- and early-morning watches.

Those were the best of times. Mary Margaret and I would sit together in the cockpit, our bodies touching as the sloop slid silently through the night and the sea wind cooled us. Despite restrictions placed on us by bodies hampered with arthritis, we made love from time to time, certainly more often than when we were ashore and living in a more mundane style.

To be sure, desire came much more slowly than when we were young. All-out passion rarely surfaced. More commonly, we prefaced our lovemaking comfortably by a long period of tender foreplay, with touching, gentle stroking and rubbing. Our lips at first would meet with simple appreciation for the decades of love and care each had given the other. Then, we would begin to press together with forces reminiscent of our youth and finally our mouths would become deep and inviting. From time to time our efforts would degenerate into giggles as

I failed to achieve my desired body state and Mary Margaret would take me to task for "building the flames but unable to throw the log on the fire." Her needles were gentle and never unkind. We preferred to face the realities of the golden years, not all of them pleasant, with understanding, love and humor.

But there were delicious times when our aging bodies responded to each other with unyielding desire and an unstoppable buildup of mutual movement and penetration that culminated in intimate muscle spasms so much more satisfying than our youthful orgasms. Sex may have been exquisite fun in those days; now, it was a sacrament.

There had been only one drawback. I carried between my legs a terrible secret, one I had never revealed to Mary Margaret and one that she could never have detected. It tormented me even to this day and there was bitterness and no forgiveness in my heart. I had tried to overcome it, but the years only brought on more regret and anger.

I did not care to dwell on that any longer. It was too beautiful a day and my annual adventure was about to begin. Niko and Sarah had already joined the others and all were milling about on the beach renewing their friendships and excitedly bringing each other up to date on the past year's happenings.

Anxious to get ashore, I stood and dived into the lagoon, allowing myself a long glide beneath the surface. The fishes instinctively gave way and only a few bothered to give me even a cursory inspection. My lungs were still strong and I breaststroked along the bottom, turning over an occasional large shell and watching the disturbed sand rise and settle. What a glorious experience! The water temperature was only a few degrees below my own.

CHAPTER 2

THE DECISION

My island manager, Sammy Kamehame, a rotund middle-aged Hawaiian from Kauai, met me at the water's edge with a huge bath towel, dry thongs and a tall Bloody Mary.

"Aah," I exclaimed in anticipation, grabbing the towel first and then stepping into the footwear. My two female staff members placed the leis over my shoulders and kissed me on the cheeks. *"Mahalo,"* I responded, then remembered we were in a Fijian mode. I added, *"Vinaka,"* and they giggled. I patted myself dry and took the Bloody Mary. "Delicious," I exclaimed, but it was not quite right. The taste was just a tad too sweet. "Not the same bartender?" I asked

Sammy laughed. "Island girl got him. She was wif a sailing canoe group dat took shelter here a few months ago from a fast moving squall. I don' know what she had as she was not one of our choicest pieces of meat in dis place. Now, we have an older gentleman for barkeep." Sammy placed his hands in a prayer position and bowed slightly as he paid his respects to age. He was only forty-four, a benevolent slave driver who oversaw the village with around-the-clock efficiency but was fair and considerate of his staff. He was a sort of Polynesian oxymoron who was both authoritative and fatherly.

"I'll have to clean up his Bloody Mary style, that's for sure," I remarked. I had a thing about Bloody Marys. There had to be sufficient Tobasco added to the mix to make me

13

smack my lips, a small splash of Worcheshire Sauce to dull the acid taste of the tomato juice and just a pinch of sugar, no more. A slice of lime *must* perch on the rim of the glass and a fresh stalk of celery must be inserted into the drink to provide a stirring tool. If they were all present in the right proportions, they wrapped the kick of the vodka within their various flavors and the result was a smooth but perky wake-up drink that started the day off just right.

"You like to meet him, now? He's in da lounge."

"I thought we didn't open that until two. I do want to walk around the island."

Sammy shrugged. "No clientele. We open for you. Dat drink not last you to lunch, I know dat."

I chuckled as I felt the tiny tingle of a small creature rushing across one of my bare feet. The sand crabs of Vaka Malua were also welcoming me back. Several of the small nervous crustaceans were darting toward the water, bent on picking up the small bits of dead fish that were a staple of their diet. Normally night-feeders, they must have been stimulated by our movements and happy chatter. I watched them in amusement for a moment as they scattered to and fro, unsure of where the choicest morsels were, their minuscule brains constantly confusing their feet.

I followed Sammy into the lounge. Behind the native wood bar, a short, slightly wrinkled Japanese man bowed in welcome to his employer. I held out my hand and received a weak but friendly grip in return.

"Dis is Nakai," Sammy introduced. "Nakai, dis Mistah Fostah."

The Japanese elder was proper but not shy. "Welcome back

14

to Vaka Malua, Mister Foster. You have beautiful place here and I thank you for opportunity to be part of it."

I was a bit disappointed with Sammy's choice. I wanted my staff to be all Polynesian or Melanesian as in the case of my Fijian dining room attendant. I had never developed any real love for the Japanese. I didn't consider myself prejudiced although, God knows, I had reason. I admired them in many ways and my business dealings with them, for the large part, had been pleasant and satisfying in the outcomes. Perhaps, I had found them to be too accommodating when engaged in public dealings but most often such an agreeable nature was a subterfuge for what was going on in their steel-trap minds. They were tough negotiators with impeccable professional manners and an astounding depth of knowledge. However, whenever I was with them, even on social occasions, I seemed to always go back to December, 1941, when their wide-smiling ambassadors in top hats and morning coats were talking peace in Washington and their fleet was sailing toward Pearl Harbor in full combat gear. Nakai looked old enough to have been a part of that generation.

I know that it was not charitable of me, but I harbored some resentment at the hordes of Japanese tourists that invaded Hawaii on a steady basis. Many of them were young honeymooners and executives whose greatest joy seemed to be filling shopping bags from Nieman Marcus and Georgio's and all of the upscale stores. I couldn't believe that they had any real sense of where they were. I also realized that in another few years it would not make any difference.

Strangely enough, I never resented their visits to the Arizona Memorial for they were almost always quiet, polite and careful to remain aware of their relationship to that beautifully bleached inverted arch mounted over the hull of the sunken battleship. They took less notice of the mighty *Missouri*, moored just aft of the *Arizona*, for it was on that warship where the Imperial dream of conquest had ended. Many of the older ones avoided looking you in the eye, but the younger ones were more like school children, reading the plaques and descriptions and the sacred names on the white marble wall of remembrance. My uncle's name was on that wall.

I also felt guilt at my automatic response to their presence because it was so contrary to the admiration and respect I had for Japanese-Americans, my fellow citizens who needed to bow their heads to no man. Despite the indignities we thrust upon them in our wartime panic, despite the humiliation of Manzanar and other internment camps, they remained one hundred percent loyal to their adopted land. They produced some of the finest fighting Americans of the war. Our country would always be in their debt.

I sat on one of the stools. "Where were you before?"

"I worked on Viti Levu at the Fiji Hilton. Bartender, as here. Before that, I was in my Japan. Hokkaido. I was very successful merchant."

"I've been on that island," I remarked. "Beautiful place with rugged coastlines and hills that test your walking stamina. Piss poor weather and cold in winter. That why you left?"

"No, I tired of progress and westernization. I am too traditional, I suppose. Many years back, I travel this area and admire its tranquillity. Sammy contact me at the Hilton when vacancy occur. There were visitors here so I must make up mind in hurry. Sammy can not even mix decent gin and tonic."

Nakai laughed as he recalled his sudden decision. "I think good career move, *hai?*"

"*Hai*," I replied, spontaneously returning the ever-present Japanese word for the affirmative.

"Oh, you speak Japanese, *hai?*"

I held up my hands in defense. "Only a few words, Nakai. Really just ones left over from the early fifties when I was a businessman in your country. *Hai, skoshi, misu, doso, arigato, konnichiwa*, that kind of stuff." There was no need to tell him I was fluent in his language.

"You have been in Nippon several times?"

"Yes...several times," I remarked slowly, staring at my drink, my mind suddenly propelled back to my first visit—in 1945. Sammy seemed to recognize that it was an awkward moment for me and motioned for Nakai to build me another drink.

I shook my head. "No, this will do." A pleasant look returned to my face. "I need to talk to you about the subtleties of Bloody Marys. This is very good but maybe a little less sugar would be perfect."

Nakai was all grin. "I fix that for you. No problem."

"Sammy, I'd like to take that walkaround before the sun gets too high."

"I'll go wif you, boss. We better take hats and water."

It would be a good two-to-three-hour walk around the sandy perimeter of Vaka Malua, probably an eight-mile distance since the small island was about one and a half miles in diameter. I always liked to make an inspection first thing after arrival. It not only gave me a chance to see that the island was being maintained properly but it afforded me a view of practically all of the lagoon. It was quite large, the surrounding coral reef a good

17

twenty-five miles or so in length. Also enclosed were several tiny islets, each only suitable for picnics or diving bases.

At the general store, I chose a wide-brimmed straw "islander's" hat while Sammy grabbed his white baseball cap. We each took full canteens. I had made sure that the village had a modern distilling system and the water was safe to drink, even from the faucets. Niko had returned to the *Mary Margaret* and retrieved some clothing and toilet articles for me. I changed into khaki shorts, a loose cotton shirt and sandals.

For no particular reason we choose a clockwise route from the south beach and within forty minutes were on the west beach. It was as pristine as that fronting the village but not as frequently used. In fact, there was a continuous strip of white unsoiled sand around the entire island, interrupted only by a small inlet on the north shore where a group of mangrove trees had taken root. Their exposed legs jutted out over the water for a foot or so before bending down to the bottom of the lagoon.

"Still some crabs here?" I queried as we reached the area some thirty minutes later. The large, thick-shelled Mangrove Crabs were one of the few gourmet delights available on Vaka Malua.

"We still get a few. I don' want to deplete dem too much or dey die out. We get most of dem for da guests from one of da odda islands."

I walked inland a few steps to get some shade. I had not hiked any appreciable distance in a while, having spent the last two weeks aboard the confines of the *Mary Margaret*. The water in the canteen was still cool and refreshing. I was immediately renewed. We were approximately at the midpoint in our walk. "How much do you know about Nakai?" I asked.

"Only about wot he tol' you. I had met him several times before on supply runs. Da Hilton people spoke well of him. I had to offer him good money to get him on such short notice."

I nodded. I expected to pay my people well. "How old is he?"

"Don' know. Probably in his late sixties but very agile and a hard worker. He's refinished da whole back of da bar in da two months he's been wif us. Looks a lot bettah."

"Yes, I noticed that. Very Melanesian even if done by a Japanese."

"He knows deese islands and da culture."

"Well, he seems cheerful enough. As long as he's a good listener and keeps our guests happy and plied with good liquor, I guess he'll do well. I do have some reservations. I instinctively seemed to dislike him. That's unusual for me. For some reason, he did not strike me as a bartender, at least one that old tending bar out here."

"He's professional, believe me."

"I do. But it's strange. Weird. I seemed to recognize his face. It was immediate, almost shocking but I can't place him."

"Talk to him. He would like dat. Maybe you find some common ground, maybe where you met befo'. It could have been when you were on your business trips to Japan. You said you were on Hokkaido. He was a merchant dere."

"No, my contacts there were well up on corporate ladders. He's nice enough but doesn't have their polish."

"Well, boss, we Hawaiians always say of da Japanese, 'dey all look alike.'"

"God knows there are enough of them on Oahu." Realizing how that statement might sound, I quickly added, "The tourists, I'm speaking of."

"Dey spend da bucks."

"That they do." I felt uncomfortable. The cult of political correctness laid that guilt trip on you whenever you spoke of other ethnic groups even if the statement were completely innocuous. But I was not satisfied with the hiring of Nakai although I knew that it had been a matter of some urgency.

I wanted Sammy to be aware of my feelings. "I think we should replace Nakai as soon as convenient. If you need a reason, it's just that I prefer to keep the staff Polynesian."

"Certainly, boss. I understand."

I knew Sammy didn't really understand but he did not have to. "Let's go on," I said.

We maintained a leisurely pace and I could see that the island and the lagoon, if anything, were healthier than before. I supposed I should have felt guilty at keeping such a place primarily to myself but hey, God had given all of Eden to just two people.

Two hours and half-a-canteen of water after we had left the village we were at the east end of north beach. The last mile had seen an increase in the tall, slim coconut palms, curved inland from the prevailing winds and loaded with their hard fruit. There was heavier ground cover and several kinds of flora not found on the west side. The east end of Vaka Malua was the high end, the ancient rim segment of its parent volcano rising an impressive four hundred feet. In the hollow of the rim, there was a healthy stand of bamboo with trunks varying in diameter from one to eight inches. Most of the village building materials had come from there and young shoots were already replacing those sections.

"I always liked this end," I remarked. "The volcano rim reminds me of the hellish upheaval of molten lava that gave

20

birth to this island and I can see God's creation in the conversion of such a catastrophic act of nature into a thing of beauty. It's a great place for meditation. Mary Margaret and I used to walk here, the short way of course, and we would watch the sea beyond the reef from high on the rim there. We'd bring a picnic lunch, a little Early Times and a canteen of water." I grinned at Sammy. "Sometimes, there would even be a little hanky-panky."

Sammy raised his hands in mock shock. "I can't see Miss Mary out here in da open...ah...playin' around. Y'know what I'm sayin'?"

"Hey, we were younger then and the juices still flowed readily. We were husband and wife and this is a very secluded area. Hell, in those days, right after I'd bought the island, we were the only ones on it. It was Paradise, Sammy. It still is. We had our own powerboat over on Viti Levu and we'd motor over for a couple days at a time. Mary Margaret used to say that Adam and Eve had a pretty good gig going for them if they had not wanted it all. Vaka Malua was our Eden and we did have it all. But God didn't toss us out. He knew we were just too right for one another. I'll always thank Him for that. Incidentally, you're a healthy young man. How does being in my service out here fit in with your natural urges? "

Sammy grinned. "Me an' da maid have a little thing going."

"Leoa? Not a good idea. Management and labor, you know."

"It's strictly physical. She's close to my age and her husband left her years ago. She misses things. No commitment, just a roll on da beach from time t' time. It don' happen very often. She puts in heavy days when guests are here and I have my own responsibilities. I can cut it off if you like—da rela-

21

tionship, dat is. I don' want to jeopardize my job."

"Give it a try, Sammy. I don't think it's a good thing—from the business standpoint. Just make a few extra supply trips to Viti Levu."

"You got it, boss."

We were coming onto the south shore and the village was a couple hundred yards ahead. It looked good, true to Melanesian style and construction with the high peaked dwellings all roofed with heavy thatch, even the boathouse, which was just ahead. It protected an eighteen-footer available for unscheduled supply trips or possible emergency runs. Those would be unlikely with Viti Levu being only twelve minutes away by helicopter. The hospital there always maintained a ready chopper in case it was needed on any of the outer islands. I had entertained thoughts about putting my own rotary-winged craft on Vaka Malua but it really wasn't needed and it would bring too much of the technical world into Paradise. I would not allow any type of power boat except for the eighteen-foot safety craft and it was kept out of sight. If my infrequent guests wanted to explore the lagoon, there were canoes and paddleboards. The village did maintain one large outrigger, which was available to take small parties out to the islets for picnics or diving. It was seldom used since most of the guests, being my contemporaries, were at the age where nursing Mai Tais and watching the sunsets were in themselves strenuous activities.

As we walked along, I wondered if I should expand, make a real resort out of Vaka Malua now that Mary Margaret was gone. I could easily see thirty or so cottages along south beach and a large central ceremonial hut where we could bring in

22

local entertainers and have a gift shop and a hairdresser and....to hell with all that. Vaka Malua would become just another tourist trap with woodcraft made in Taiwan. I chuckled inwardly. I was thinking like an active businessman. I really didn't want that anymore.

I gazed down south beach. Even my small development detracted from its natural beauty. Such a place should be preserved. I could scale it down, take away a couple of the *bures*, perhaps. I could not recall a single instance when all five had been occupied at the same time. I know that some of my past guests had not been too careful around the native foliage. Mary Margaret had even cautioned me about making too much of it.

"Leave it just for us," she had suggested. Now that she was gone, it was even more special to me.

Her words came back again. I *had* intended to keep Vaka Malua for just us, allowing a few friends to enjoy it merely to cover overhead. But we had so little time to enjoy it before the beast devoured her. The island and the lagoon that held her ashes were the most precious possession I now had. At that precise moment, I decided I would keep Vaka Malua all to myself and dedicate it's purity to Mary Margaret. In fact —and the thought came to me in a unexpected flash —I was not ever going to leave it again! I would stop renting out the overwater *bures* and gradually release my staff. Yes, yes. I would have to keep someone around, perhaps, in the event I became ill or injured but even those possibilities could be covered by a reliable communications link with Viti Levu and I already had that.

I had tasted and thoroughly enjoyed the life of the open sea with its simple requirements for existence. But lately, if I were being completely honest with myself, I had found that bad weather and the stress of sailing in less than ideal conditions were no longer challenging to me, just a bit frightful. It was hard to confess such a thing to myself.

I could ride out any weather on Vaka Malua. If a storm took away my *bures*, I had a large bamboo stand with which to rebuild. I was still in reasonably good health and could put in a day's work if it weren't too demanding. The sea air that bathed the island, with its smell of salt and seaweed, was my fountain of youth, even an aphrodisiac. Sadly, I realized that the latter quality was of no use to me any longer.

The more I thought of it, the more I knew that Vaka Malua was my destiny. Something, yet undiscovered, had brought me here.

As for the isolation, I didn't need people. I had enough of people, except for the Polynesians. I loved their appreciation of the sea and the islands, especially those away from the tourist developments that had turned so many islands into a series of theme-park Polynesialands where too often the dancers wore colorful plastic grass skirts and high-rise buildings hid the mountains and rain forests. That was sacrilegious, even if inevitable. If I could save one tiny part of planet Earth, I would have accomplished much and it would give me a valuable purpose in life. My friends would say I'd gone native for sure. I didn't care. I loved the Pacific peoples.

I loved the Hawaiians for their love of life itself, their luaus and hukilaus, their music and hulas, their carefree life style where party was king and food was "all time da best."

The Tahitians, on the other hand, were the sensual ones, the women most joyful when dancing, their rapidly oscillating hips capable of driving the Pope mad. The men knew they

24

were the most blessed of all Polynesians. In their pure state they fished, napped, ate and made love. In their tourist mode, they made visitors wish to remain in Tahiti forever. If I were twenty years younger, I would seek out a place in Tahiti.

I had a special place in my heart for the Maoris of New Zealand. Their fierce, tattooed faces, rolling eyes, and thrusting tongues gave them every appearance of being deadly warriors who would slay you and eat you in a second. Really, they preferred to chant, sing and dance with their women, and to recount their old days when they truly did relish tribal warfare.

As for the Marquesas, the gentle Polynesians accustomed to French rule, they were graceful in dance, modest in dress and adapted to progress while at the same time maintaining their culture.

There were the Tonganese and the Samoans, darker than the Hawaiians but not the Fijians. They were fun-loving and muscular, their dances energetic responses to their loud, aggressive, warlike music. To them, a hollow log was a thousand instruments, depending upon how it was beaten.

Finally, the Melanesian Fijians captivated me with their childlike playfulness and their spirited three-part harmony and impish fire-walks where ritual was accented by comedy and tradition passed by English explanations of everything that went on at such exciting ceremonies. These black people of the Pacific were modest and courteous and perhaps the most hospitable of them all.

I could do much worse than to live out my life among such people.

Sammy excused himself as we reached the village, "If dere's nothing else for da moment, boss, I promised Manalo I

25

would help him with da plumbing in number four. Dere's some blockage somewhere."

Manalo was a native Tahitian, tall, lean, twentyish and one of those rare analytical individuals who could cope with almost any material problem although he had only a grade school education. He was also one of the few Polynesians I had met who could still navigate a canoe across the horizon and find fish where there were apparently none. When not tied to his repair and upkeep duties, he could usually be found out in the open sea just beyond the lagoon entrance, fishing and quaffing a six-pack in the hot sun. He never failed to provide fresh snapper or red fish or some other good eating fish for the tables. Often when he took the eighteen-footer, he would bring back trophy-sized *ahi* for the kitchen. He could also be counted on for shark but don't ask him to walk across the island and bring back a sturdy, thick-shelled mangrove crab. That was woman's work.

I walked on down to the westernmost *bure*. That one was mine and I took stock of the things Niko had brought ashore from the *Mary Margaret*. It was close to noon but the screened-in *bure* allowed a crosscurrent of sea air and an overhead fan provided a downward thrust. I switched it to high.

The *Mary Margaret* rode quietly at anchor visible from here. Beyond her, I sighted several other sailing craft passing south of Vaka Malua, their pointed sails full of the trade wind. One even had a billowing red spinnaker ballooning out over its bow, making a downwind run. I judged its speed to be an impressive twenty knots. That would be Charlie Dobson, the manager of the Fiji Hilton. Where was he off to on this Friday? The hotel provided continuous entertainment and tours. The weekends were his busiest times.

I counted five boats in all; five little sailing craft on this vast ocean, and none of them interested in my island. That's the way I liked it.

The shower water was not cool but it was wet. When I finished and stepped out to towel myself dry, the net result was that I was as wet as before. The humidity must be at least ninety percent; there were lots of clouds around. In all probability, Vaka Malua would take its own shower in the late evening. For the moment, I was content to stand under the overhead fan and allow its draft to cool me. I was refreshed after the hot walk and when I lay on the waterbed I felt the delicious relaxation of an approaching nap.

Let's rest, Mary Margaret, I thought to myself. *We've done enough for this morning.*

Strangely, I didn't drop off immediately. My mind searched the vaguely familiar features of Nakai's Japanese face, particularly the deep-set eyes. I was disturbed at his presence. I knew him. Where? Where had it been?

Finally, it was just too quiet and I was too comfortable to remain awake. The image of Nakai's face dissolved. I closed my eyes.

I remember dreaming of Mary Margaret and getting up to urinate but I'm not certain I know what happened next. I was in deep sleep. I dreamed a series of nightmarish vignettes but everything was confused. I'd had similar dreams before but this one was in considerable detail and deeply disturbing. I woke up with my own screams echoing in my ears, but my voice seemed to be detached from my body. "No, stay away!" I was pleading. "Oh, God, don't let him hurt me again!"

I was curled in one corner of the *bure* and there were fig-

27

ures around me. I tried to recognize them but I couldn't bring their faces into focus. I didn't want them to hurt me anymore. "Please, stay away!" I begged. I could hardly breathe.

Someone grabbed me and tried to pull me from the corner. It was Nakai, but he was not strong enough. Manalo helped him and together they got me onto the bed. Sammy joined the two men, and all three held me down while Leoa ran into the bathroom area and returned with a wet towel. Nakai searched through the toilet articles on the nightstand, probably hoping to find some medication that would be labeled "Take as needed." In his mind, I suspected, I had certainly experienced some form of attack. There was only one prescription drug: digitalis. I had a controllable heart problem but Nakai seemed to know that particular medicine would be of no help at the moment.

Slowly, some signs of sanity began to return. "Nakai?" I asked. "Leoa." I managed a very weak grin, comforted by the familiar faces. "I'm sorry. This sometimes happens to me. It's nothing."

"Nothing, boss?" Sammy repeated. "We need to get you to da doctah."

"No. It's all right, really it is...this has happened before and it has all been explained to me. Something to drink, maybe."

My *bure*, like all the others, had a small office-sized refrigerator. Leoa retrieved a bottle of guava juice and poured it into a glass.

"Thank you." I was calm but my breathing was still labored and I was saturated with sweat. I sat up to drink and seemed to be steady. "Last time was four years ago," I said quietly. "I thought it was all over."

"All what was ovah?" Sammy asked.

"What time is it?" I interrupted.

"Two-twenty-two, sir" answered Manalo. The young Tahitian was visibly shaken. Since he no longer needed to hold me on the bed, he had retreated several steps.

"I'm all right, now." I was really feeling better. "Please, go on about your business. Thank you all."

Sammy was still concerned. "Let me sit with you a while, boss."

"No, I'll be fine." I just needed to wash my face.

❋   ❋   ❋

I had been left in my *bure* at my insistence. I saw no one until late afternoon when I walked into the lounge and took a table near the railing where I could look out over the lagoon.

Nakai approached me. "Drink, sir?"

"Yes. Bourbon and water. Thank you, Nakai."

"You looking better."

"I'm feeling fine. I apologize for the disruption."

"It was nothing. We were all concerned."

Sammy Kamehame walked in. "Good to see da color's back."

"I'm glad you're here, Sammy. Sit down. I'd like to talk for a moment."

Sammy somehow stuffed his nearly three-hundred pounds into one of the captain's chairs that were arranged around all of the tables. Nakai returned with my drink and a Diet Coke™ for Sammy.

"Sammy, I may live a hundred years. Who knows? I may not make it through tomorrow. But, whatever my time is, I want to spend it here. I love the islands. I love the people. I can never become one of you; I'll always be a *haole*. But on Vaka Malua, I'll be as close as I can get."

"Boss, you already *kamaaina*." Grinning, Sammy added, "I think you make bettah Hawaiian dan Fijian but dat your choice. Long time ago, we all come from somewhere else."

It was true that I was very familiar with the islands of Polynesia, having sailed them for fifteen years. My land home on Oahu stood at the water's edge below Diamond Head.

"Well, anyhow, I'm dropping anchor right here, today. I'm not going back to Honolulu. I want you to call the staff together after dinner, here in the lounge and I'll tell them. I'd appreciate it if you wouldn't say anything until then."

"You got it, boss." Sensing I had said all I was going to say, Sammy excused himself and headed for his office.

I finished my bourbon and let my mind merge with the waters of the lagoon. I was incredibly at peace with myself, even after the disturbing memories that had shattered my earlier nap. Maybe the cathartic dreams had actually played a part in my sudden decision.

And I was convinced that it was a good decision. There comes a time in a person's life, if that person has Christian beliefs, when he or she wants to set aside some time to prepare for the next world. I had a lot of preparing to do, for although I had been raised in a religious family, I had lost my youthful enthusiasm after the war. I had been disillusioned, surely. But primarily it had been my complete emergence into the business world and the realization that I was capable of making a lot of money that distanced me from my faith. In my worship of the dollar, I didn't feel I had broken the First Commandment but I sure had bent the hell out of it. I shared my good fortune with a number of charities, of course, but my motivation had been driven more by the taxation system than a philosophy of giving.

Whatever the case, I knew now that Vaka Malua had been waiting for me like a patient priest since I had come home from the war over fifty years ago. Everything in between had been filler. My professional drive had made me a rich man. My wife had made me a blessed man. But my memories had made me an incomplete man.

I carried horrible scars on my body and in my head that denied me the ability to forgive and forget. They were too deep and every day they hurt like hell. *Every* day. And at times, like today, I dreamed about my demon.

For some unfathomable, completely irrational reason, I knew that Vaka Malua would provide a solution to my intensely private shame and pain. Even my beloved wife's passing had been an instrument to drive me here.

I left my *bure* and strolled down to the edge of the lagoon. I stared at the calm water and lifted my arms to let the breeze cool my chest and armpits. With so little surf, there was only a soft lapping sound and an almost imperceptible rustle and muted clatter of the scurrying sand crabs.

I could feel the presence of my beloved wife. *Okay. Mary Margaret, you were always so far ahead of me in our life together. What's next?*

CHAPTER 3

PREPARATIONS

The assembled staff was anxious to hear what I had to say. Most were seated, but Sammy and Nakai stood nervously by the bar. Was it going to be criticism of their work? Praise would be good, and I was known to be free with that when it was warranted.

Leoa seemed to be uncomfortable. Perhaps Sammy had told her that they should cut off their relationship after our talk. Surely, he had not been dumb enough to admit to her that he had spoken of it to me. Still, something was wrong. She stared at Sammy until she caught his eye, and shot a volley of mental female daggers at the hapless Polynesian. He winced unconsciously as they stabbed into with an invisible fury of which only Sammy was fully aware. He quickly averted his gaze to the lagoon although he knew that I would be speaking of an entirely different subject. I dismissed my thought as their problem, not mine.

"I have made a rather abrupt decision," I began. "It affects all of us, so I thought it best to inform you right away. I have decided to take up permanent residence on Vaka Malua."

Leoa visibly relaxed.

I glanced from eye to eye briefly, and continued. "You have all made this place what it is, an island paradise home for me and Mary Margaret when she was alive and a most pleasant getaway for our guests. However, I prefer to retire here alone. I will no longer need your services after I get my affairs in order. That will require a trip to Viti Levu and I'll be going over there Monday morning. Manalo, I'd like you to have the eighteen-footer ready."

"Yes, sir."

"Each of you will receive the rest of your contract salaries plus six months severance pay. If there is any particular hardship that needs to be addressed, please see Sammy before Monday. I'm sure we can work something out."

I did not want to drag this on. These were my friends as well as my employees and I knew they had been unprepared for my announcement.

"With that in mind, please feel free to leave any time after the middle of the week. The supply boat will be here Thursday, as you know, or Manalo can take you over to Viti Levu if you need to leave sooner."

I scanned the faces. This was much harder than I had thought it would be. These people had been very loyal to me and given me a full measure of work for each day's pay. Nakai, particularly, seemed to be concerned, and he had only been in my service for a relatively short while.

"Nakai, I'm certain the Hilton will want you right back."

"That would be nice."

"I'll speak to Mister Dobson. Are there any questions?"

Manalo must have remembered the look of terror on my face just a few hours earlier and also the weakness of my body as I had fought with my demon. "Sir, are you sure you don't want someone to stay with you, at least for a while? I would be pleased to. Just until you know things are going well."

"I think dat would be wise, boss," Sammy chimed in. "I be glad t' stay."

34

"No, I need to get right into it." Even as I spoke, I was having some second thoughts. I really didn't intend to keep the guest *bures* serviceable. They would have to be dismantled and the area cleaned up. Physically, that might be beyond me. Besides, I could more quickly convert the main hut to my needs. It would not need any drastic changes. Also, there would be no reason to keep the staff quarters although they were back away from the beachfront, secluded among the trees and hidden from direct view. Vaka Malua should be returned as closely as possible to its former pristine state. I was about to accept Manalo's offer when it occurred to me that Niko and Sarah would be the better choices. I felt very close to them and their contract was open ended. It would also mean that I might not have to sacrifice my love for sailing, cold turkey. Yes, that should be the plan.

"I'll keep Niko and Sarah with me for a short while." I knew there would be some noses out of joint on that decision but I had made such calls before. You weighed the options and took the best one. Sammy could never do a full day's physical work, much less a week or so. The two women would not be needed. The cook should try to find a position on Viti Levu as soon as practical. There were good opportunities there. And Manalo should get on with his life. He was young, intelligent, hardworking and eager to please. Fiji might not be the place for him but I could see to the completion of his education on Oahu. With his quick mind and analytical way of thinking problems through, Manalo could succeed in any profession he chose to enter. I would gladly pick up the tab and the Tahitian would be a natural for the work-study program at the Mormon's Polynesian Cultural Center on the north shore of Oahu. We would talk Monday on the way over to Viti Levu.

There was no reason to keep my people any longer. "Thank all of you," I said. I dismissed them with a nod.

I would need to talk to Niko and Sarah. They were undoubtedly out on the *Mary Margaret,* although I had offered them the use of one of the *bures.* I could see the cabin lights as well as the anchor lights reflecting off the placid waters of the lagoon. Although I didn't consider the anchor lights necessary in such a private lagoon, it was required by the International Rules of the Road. Just so long as Niko kept the batteries charged, it was probably the wisest configuration.

The night was warm and there were a million jillion stars overhead. A full moon sprayed silver over the ocean beyond the reef and the lagoon was as still as a Wyeth painting. I wished I were more artistic, but I acknowledged that no brush could capture what lay before me.

I left my shirt and sandals on the beach and slipped into the water. The impression was that I had returned to the womb and its life-giving embryonic fluid. The water caressed my skin, comfortable and all-embracing. I felt as if I could swim all the way back to Hawaii but the *Mary Margaret* was obviously a better choice.

I didn't stroke the water. I returned its caress. My hands pulled it beneath me with steady, graceful movements, cupping just enough to give me that extra pull. My body cut the surface of the lagoon as easily as the hull of my sloop. After several strokes, I rolled over on my back and looked beyond my feet at the village. The torches were lit and the only electric light was that from the lounge. It was obscene and out of place. There should be only natural light on Vaka Malua. It would be

36

so, once I settled in. I would keep the electrical system but it would be used only as necessary, not on a regular basis.

I was halfway to the sloop and far enough out that I could hear the ocean crashing against the reef, angry and frustrated that it could not tear away the coral. It was not a high sea and only a few waves threw themselves upward far enough to swirl across the reef. They filled the crevices with rivulets of white foam that bled back into the ocean. Very little water crossed the reef and made it into the lagoon.

I stopped and treaded water, listening to the sounds. I was in the middle of a great Pacific opera where the crash of the waves provided entrance music for a diva who would never show. The heavy curtain of the night would not rise, burdened as it was by the endless array of sparkling diamonds. The floodlight of the moon waited patiently, a wide wisp of gossamer across the heavens. It was about all the beauty that the human eye could take in at any one time.

I resumed my swim, returning once more to a lazy backstroke, letting my feet do most of the work. My eyes tried to measure the unmeasurable distance to the stars. I would certainly sleep this night.

So absorbed was I that I forgot I was closing on the *Mary Margaret*. The sharp rap of my head against the hull reminded me.

"Ahoy!" I sang out in my best seagoing voice, "Ahoy, aboard the *Mary Margaret*!" I heard the scurry of bare feet and Niko's head appeared over the rail. He was clad in only his shorts and I suspected that Sarah wore even less. It was that kind of night.

"Skipper! What are you doing out here? You planning on swimming over to Viti Levu?"

"Hi, Niko. I just felt I needed a nightcap and seawater seemed like the right thing."

Niko dropped a short boarding ladder over the side. "We got something much better than that."

As he helped me onto the deck, Sarah came up from below, clad in a halter and shorts. Her hair was in mild disarray and she ran her fingers through it to coax it into some sense of order. "Captain, what a pleasant surprise. We were going to take the Zodiac in later on to see how you were doing."

I'll bet you were, I thought, trying not to let my face betray my amusement. Only one button on the side of her shorts was fastened.

We passed down the short companionway into the salon. The side portholes were open as was the forward window and there was a comfortable cross-breeze.

"Bourbon and water, skipper?" Niko asked.

"As always," I responded.

Sarah had edged her way forward and was trying to discreetly close the hatch to the bow stateroom but I got a quick glimpse at the linen which looked like it had just weathered a force-three tropical storm. The sheets probably *had* been through a rough ride and I felt a bit of guilt at interrupting.

"Niko, Sarah, this has been quite a day for me. I won't go into details but I've decided to settle here on Vaka Malua."

Niko handed me my drink. "Settle? Like forever?"

"Well, as long as forever is for me in this world."

"That's great," Sarah exclaimed. "Vaka Malua is you."

"I would like to keep you two around for a short while, long enough for you, Niko, to dismantle the *bures* and clean up a few other items. I might want the staff quarters to be razed."

"No problem, skipper."

"When the time comes, I'll want you to take the *Mary Margaret* back to Honolulu and sell her. I'll make it worth your while, of course, and see that you receive just compensation for all your time with me. Niko, you and Sarah have been the children Mary Margaret and I never had."

"That will be a sad time, sir."

"No, Niko, it will be a happy time. I will finally have determined my destiny and you with Sarah can begin a life ashore. You've spent enough time at sea with a couple of old toads. It's time for children and the special joys they bring."

Sarah reached over and lightly grasped one of Niko's hands.

I looked at the two. Their children would be Polynesian gods or goddesses; such was the beauty of my two Pacific friends. Perhaps, one day in the not too distant future, they would visit me on Vaka Malua and I could hold the little ones and take them down to the waters edge and point out the fishes.

I finished most of my bourbon. "Well, I wanted you to know right away. I'll be over on Viti Levu on Monday, probably Suva. Most of the staff will be gone by Thursday. Move into one of the *bures*. You'll be more comfortable and it'll be the last thing we dismantle."

Niko stood. "I'll take you back in the Zodiac."

"No, I'm not tired at all. The water is perfect tonight."

Niko and Sarah followed me to the rail and I dove over the side.

I should have jumped in feet first. For a confusing moment, I lost all sense of up and down. There was little light beneath the surface, only that provided by the bright moon. Age was having an effect upon my sensory perception ability and I spent

39

an anxious moment before I determined my attitude. Relieved, I surfaced and began a leisurely breaststroke toward shore.

❀ ❀ ❀

Saturday and Sunday were precursors of life to come. I puttered around the main hut, making mental plans about how I would arrange it for permanent residency. I chatted with the various staff members and I could see that they were rapidly adapting to the situation. None seemed to have any particular problems, although all were clearly disappointed at having to make the unexpected change in their lifestyle.

I insisted they join me Sunday evening for a farewell dinner. Niko and Sarah had moved into their *bure* and Sarah took over the cooking chores while Niko tended bar and served the staff and me.

It was a good night. Sammy made sure that Polynesian music flowed from the dining area sound system and he and Leoa danced several hulas including a comic rendition to the classic "Cockeyed Mayor of Kanakakai." Manalo surprised us all with a fierce Tahitian love dance, at one point pulling Leoa onto the floor and gyrating around her with rapid, highly seductive thigh movements and hip thrusts that brought forth laughter and spontaneous applause from the others. The dance ended with Leoa pulling Manalo into her ample bosom and pleading, "Kiss me, kiss me!" The struggling Manalo responded with, "Help me, I can't breathe!"

I excused myself shortly after eleven but I could hear the winding down of the party from my *bure*. It was a pleasant noise, mostly happy talk punctuated with bursts of rippling

40

laughter. Sammy had most probably told another of his stories. I had never known a man with such a comic talent.

The final sounds brought tears to my eyes. Niko and Sarah were softly singing the same Hawaiian folk song they had rendered when I had spread Mary Margaret's ashes on the lagoon. I slipped off with wet cheeks to my third night of deep, uninterrupted, peaceful sleep.

By nine on Monday morning, I was comfortably seated in the stern of the eighteen-footer as Manalo piloted the husky cabin cruiser across the choppy water towards Viti Levu. It would be about a forty-five minute trip and the boat bounced and surged as it sped toward the largest Fijian island with its capital city of Suva. Only nearby Vanua Levu was of comparable size. The other 318 islands of the Republic of Fiji contributed less than half the total area of the Melanesian island nation.

"Tell me, Manalo, have you ever had any desire to further your education?" I asked.

"Oh yes, Mister Foster. But I can't afford that, not now. Besides, I'm happy out here. There are plenty of jobs. If not, I can go back to Tahiti."

"Manalo, you are an unusual young man. You obviously love life but I sense you are ambitious. You want more for yourself."

"Everybody does that, Mister Foster."

"No, not everybody. I want to do something for you."

"That's not necessary, Mister Foster."

We ducked in unison as the boat plowed into a particularly large wave and water cascaded over the bow.

"If you could be anything you wanted, what would you be?"

Manalo laughed, "Anything? An anthropologist. I would

41

like to learn more about my people, other than our stories and legends."

"Brigham Young on Oahu has such a course of study."

"I could not afford that. Besides, I am not a Mormon."

I shrugged. "So, you convert, at least for a while. You attend Brigham Young, work in the Cultural Center to help pay your way and I'll pick up all other expenses. How's that sound?"

Manalo kept his gaze across the bow. "I couldn't let you do that."

Exactly the answer I expected. Manalo was a proud young man. "Consider it a loan, interest free. Pay me back if you feel you must. But I prefer it to be a grant, a grant from a friend who feels you are capable of accomplishing good things. Mary Margaret and I had no children. Let me do this for you."

"Can I think about it?"

"Certainly. It's an open offer. And while I'm in Suva, I'm going to open an account for you in the Bank of Hawaii."

"I would rather you wouldn't."

"I'm a stubborn old man, Manalo. I have no heirs. I have too much money to spend before I go. I want to do some good for people I feel deserve it. I don't know a lot of young people."

Manalo turned and grinned. "Suppose I just piss it away."

"You won't."

There had been a red sunrise and the wind was already beginning to gust. After all, the old sailors ode, "Red sky in the morning, sailor's take warning; red sky at night, sailor's delight," was most often correct. I had no doubt that the late afternoon would bring rain squalls. I would want to be back on Vaka Malua by then.

I maintained a small suite at the Fiji Hilton and the manager, Charlie Dobson, had dispatched one of the hotel cars to pick me up at the marina. I could conduct most of my business from the suite although a visit to the Suva main branch of the National Bank of Fiji would be required to have them handle some arrangements with my bank in Honolulu. That would also give me the chance to establish Manalo's account.

Suva was its usual busy self, its 75,000 inhabitants seemingly all in the city going about their Monday morning business. As they had for years, the Indians controlled most of the financial activity, even at the lower levels of tellers and cashiers. Their ethnic group composed 48% of the Fijian population but the Fijian natives, although still a minority, were in firm control. The 1992 coup by General Sitiveni Rabuka had returned the governmental authority to the Melanesian population.

I wished I had time to call on Rabuka; we had been friends since I had contributed substantial funds to the general during the coup. But my personal needs would have to take priority this time. I could still write Rabuka a note to advise him that the republic soon would have a new citizen.

By two in the afternoon I had finished with my business, including the meeting with bank officials in Suva, and a late lunch in my suite with the hotel manager. While dining, I had asked about Nakai.

"We would be very glad to take him back. He has been a fixture in the hotel and guests are always asking about him," Dobson declared.

"He fit right in with my people."

"He would. Agreeable personality," Dobson remarked.

"I just seem to know him from somewhere."

"Nakai's that kind of man. Rare for a Japanese. Especially

a World War Two vet."

"He was in their military?"

"Imperial Japanese Army. Doesn't talk about it," Dobson commented. "You were, too, weren't you, Mister Foster?"

I unconsciously bit down on my lower lip as I replied, "Marines."

Dobson laughed. "You two should have a lot to talk about!"

"That was a long time ago. I suspect neither of us would get much comfort from such a conversation. Listen, I would like to stay a while. You are always a gracious host. But I should get back to Vaka Malua before the weather sets in."

"Yes, I understand a line of squalls is heading our way. It's that time of the year. We can fly you back on the chopper if you like. It's available."

"I would appreciate that. I'll have to inform my man at the marina. We came over on the eighteen-footer."

"I'll see he gets the word. Just call my office when you are ready to leave."

"Thanks, Charlie. That'll give me a little more time to pick up a couple things here in Suva."

"It's the hotel's pleasure, Mister Foster. Come back soon."

❄ ❄ ❄

It was almost six in the early evening by the time I finished my personal business and boarded the waiting helicopter on the hotel's pad. The pilot was a ruddy middle-aged Australian, wearing a digger's hat, a twenty-year veteran of the Royal Australian Air Force who had settled in Fiji only two years back.

"I've been wantin' t' see yer place out at Vaka Malua," he

declared as we lifted and swiftly transitioned in a steep turn toward the west.

"Surely, you've flown over it."

"Only a couple times."

Now that we had some altitude, I could see the line of storms approaching from the southeast. An ugly, low, rolling cloud preceded a line of thunderstorms stretching from horizon to horizon. Vaka Malua was only thirty miles from Viti Levu and I could already pick it out, shining in the sunlight with the black skies just beyond. I gauged the distance from the roll cloud to Vaka Malua to be less than five miles. "We're cutting it close."

"Aye, that we are," agreed the Aussie, then reassured himself, "We'll beat the bloody thing. Looks mean, doesn't it?" The nose of the helicopter lowered as the pilot increased his forward speed. I did not reply but instinctively checked my watch, although the present time was not really a factor to be considered. The time enroute was the critical consideration and I was relieved to see that we were approaching my island much faster than was squall line. It was a wide one and black as a wicked midnight.

Six minutes later the pilot descended rapidly. "I'll just have time t' drop ya off. Any particular place ya want me t' land?"

"Anywhere on the south beach is fine, just so it's not too close to the *bures*."

The pilot used the white caps to judge the wind direction and made a wide sweep over the lagoon to head into it. The roll cloud was no more than a couple miles offshore and the helicopter was already being buffeted by the gusting winds. "Keep yer seat belt fastened until I tell ya. I may have t' work to keep this bloody beast on the sand. Once yer out, run like the devil

45

hisself is after ya. Git y'self out from under the blades."

The first rain was splashing against the large clear plastic front of the helicopter as the pilot swept in over the white sand, abruptly raised his nose to stop his forward motion and descended the last few feet in a remarkably steady condition.

I could see Sammy Kamehame running out to meet us.

The helicopter skids touched and the Aussie dropped his collective and throttled back. "Now or never, Mister Foster! Stye low!" The strong, gusting winds could cause the main rotor blades to drop dangerously. With a continuous motion, I unsnapped my belt, opened the door, grabbed my packages, and jumped out. Sammy helped me slam it shut and we both gave the pilot a thumbs up.

He didn't wait. With a great blast of downwash the bird lifted off and headed for Viti Levu at wavetop level. His ride back would be even bumpier than the coming, but he should have no trouble beating the storm to Suva.

The sun disappeared, swallowed by the roll cloud. The few seabirds that had not flown away took shelter in the thick foliage of the rain forest. The cloud rolled over the island.

Sammy grabbed one of the packages from me and yelled, "We better run for it!" I didn't need further encouragement.

The sky was black above us and the winds were increasing by the second, the bursts so strong that I was almost blown over as we ran toward the dining area. A solid wall of rain bore down on us and we barely made it to the main building before the full fury of the storm struck. We were both soaked.

Sammy had lowered and secured the bamboo windbreaks but one section at the far end of the dining area took off on the stiffening wind for parts unknown. Fortunately, the unprotected section was downwind so little water was coming in. Nakai worked behind the bar to remove all the bottles of liquor from the shelves and store them in the low cabinets behind the counter.

Once I got my breath back, I asked, "Is Manalo back?"

"No, boss."

"Call the hotel marina and if he hasn't left, have them hold him there. He could never make it now."

Nakai sat two fingers of bourbon and a small glass of water before me. "You cut that one close," he remarked.

"Tell me about it. As soon as we were in the air I looked over here and had some serious reservations. The pilot was an experienced Aussie but I think he knew he had shaved it pretty thin. We were lucky."

The building shook and surged under the vicious winds that were doing their best to take it apart, but the roof maintained its integrity. Here, inside the bar/dining area, it was dry and actually cozy. I had not had time to check on the *Mary Margaret* and Sammy anticipated my next question. He had just finished his call to the hotel marina. "Manalo's still on Viti Levu. Niko's on da *Mary Margaret* and she's ridin' fine."

"Sarah with him?"

"No, she's over in da staff hut."

I took a healthy swig of my bourbon and chased it with the water. "I bet we've got fifty knots out there."

"We've had more," Sammy responded. "Everything here is well built. We can ride it out."

"Do we have a choice?" I asked. It was my first time on Vaka Malua when bad weather had struck.

"No," answered Sammy.

The rain became torrential and I found a certain satisfaction in the force of its coming, a reminder of the ultimate power of Nature and the insignificant place of Man when Nature vented its fury. Even as the winds shook the main hut, and I could hear parts of the thatch roof ripping off, I felt secure, much as a small child in its mother's lap when a storm was raging. Vaka Malua would take care of me.

I peered at the *Mary Margaret* through the house binoculars. The sloop was swinging around before the wind's rapidly changing direction. Niko stood at the wheel in the cockpit, a quick-release safety line around his waist in case he had to go forward on the weather deck. His right hand rested on the throttle of the diesel. Probably, he had started the engine when he realized the winds were getting strong enough to drag the anchor. He could have trouble detecting the irregular jerks that could signal movement of the anchor across the bottom. His main concern would be to keep enough power on to ease the strain on the chain and keel.

The bronze Polynesian was bare to the waist but had grabbed a rainhat to keep some of the moisture out of his eyes. Its brim was too flexible to do much good, however, and he spent a good deal of the time wiping his face and licking the deliciously pure rainwater off his lips. From time to time, I could see him tilt his head back and drink in the way of his ancestors, eagerly and fully. He seemed to be singing something and I suspect that in his mind he was far at sea standing spread-legged on an ancient voyaging canoe, riding the swells as it plowed through the white-capped waves. That was his heritage and I envied him.

The lagoon was certainly a lot less disturbed than the waters beyond the reef and there really should not be a problem. Squall lines, by their nature, are fast moving and narrow. At the moment, visibility was his main concern. I doubted that he could see the reef. Submerged within the noise of the heavy rain, his ears would have trouble hearing the waves pounding it. If the anchor did drag and it did so smoothly, he could drift into danger without knowing it.

But I had no real concern. Niko, by heredity and life-experience a master seafarer, was a descendent of the earliest people of the Pacific. He carried in his genes the signature of a people who had traveled throughout the entire Pacific Triangle—Hawaii to the north, Easter Island to the east and New Zealand to the south. He stood an alert watch. He munched a soggy sandwich, in all probability his favorite peanut butter and grape jelly. He took occasional swigs from a can of Pepsi Cola, undoubtedly diluted with the same water that had been evaporated by the sun, condensed into the great southern clouds and dropped back in the form of tropical rain for millions of years.

CHAPTER 4

THE DISCOVERY

The squall line had been the forerunner of a small tropical disturbance that extended over some sixty miles of ocean. It took the rest of the night to pass across Vaka Malua. I had waited along with the others until the wind began to diminish, and then we retired to our respective sleeping quarters. The rain continued quite heavy, but it was steady rather that torrential. It tapered off by three in the morning, and a light breeze cossetted the island. There was little we could do to assess any damage until daylight.

I woke early and surveyed the beach from my *bure*. There was very little debris, actually; much less than I expected. Some fallen palm fronds and semi-decayed coconuts littered the sand here and about. Bits of driftwood had washed ashore. The *bures* all looked sound, as did the main structure. The sky blazed a deep azure blue, the lagoon lay quiet, and the *Mary Margaret* rested silently at anchor.

Niko greeted me as I walked into the dining area, desperate for a cup of coffee. "Good morning, skipper." Sarah also sat at the table. She nodded and smiled, her mouth full of papaya.

"What time did you finally get off the *Mary Margaret?*" I asked.

"I stayed on all night. Swam in an hour or so ago. There was never any real danger."

Several of the others were also having breakfast. The regular cook had resumed his duties and Sammy Kamehame arrived as I took my place at the table. He and I sat at the table next to Niko and Sarah. Manalo was still over on Viti Levu.

"Doesn't look too bad," I commented.

"No, we can have da beach cleaned up in a few hours. Da boathouse is gone. Later on, Manalo and I will take a walk around and check da odda sides. Da staff hut took a little damage. One of da old palms fell across one end, wiped out Nakai's room. He's okay. He said he would like to leave today if da boat makes a run. Leoa, too."

"Can you handle the eighteen-footer?"

"Sure, boss."

"Well, when Manalo gets back I'd like him and Niko to start taking the furnishings out of the *bures* and storing them in the vacant staff rooms. The cook might as well go, also. Sarah can handle the kitchen. You can take the boat over this afternoon."

Of the original staff, that would leave only Martha, the Fijian dining room attendant, Sammy and Manalo.

Martha brought us papaya and toast. "Can I fix you a breakfast, Mister Foster?"

"No, this is fine."

Manalo arrived at mid-morning and docked where the boathouse used to be. He, Niko and Sammy began to clear out the *bures* while Sarah and Martha cleaned up the south beach then went over to the staff hut to help Nakai. He had gathered up his few belongings.

Later on, the cook, Leoa and Nakai cleared out their rooms and packed to leave. By late afternoon, things were mostly back as they had been before the storm.

I bid the three workers good-bye and handed each one their

separation pay envelope. Each thanked me profusely. Leoa broke down and gave me a tearful hug. Sammy had the eighteen-footer ready. I stood on the beach waving until they cleared the lagoon.

It was a smaller and very tired group that met for dinner.

After a simple meal, Sarah cleaned up the kitchen while we men talked.

"We got all da furniture stored," Sammy announced. "Manalo and I will start takin' da *bures* down tomorrow."

"Just two," I replied. "I think I'll leave the rest up, just in case. Besides, I've decided they give the beach flavor."

"What do you want us to do to the staff quarters now that they're used for stowage?" Manalo asked.

"That changes things, doesn't it? I think we leave the hut up. Later on, I'll contract with someone on Viti Levu to come over and take everything out. After today, I can see it is too big a job for us. That way, the rest of you can leave Thursday on the supply shuttle." Having second thoughts, I added, "Let's even forget about the *bures*." I hoped that my comment would not offend them. I knew they were anxious about me getting settled and had reservations about my ability to go it alone.

"We'll be ready," was all Sammy said.

Sarah came out from the kitchen. She placed a metal box in front of me. "Nakai must have forgotten this. Martha found it in his room when she checked it. It's locked and probably has personal papers in it. It could be valuable to him."

I examined it. It was green, about the size to hold such things, and closed with a simple turnkey lock. "No key?"

"No, sir. It's a little messy in there from the fallen tree but he could have it on his key chain," Sarah replied.

"Well, set it on the bar. I'll see that he gets it the next time I go over."

"We could take it to him Thursday," Sammy volunteered.

"Sure; he would appreciate that." Even as I spoke, I knew that the box was not leaving Vaka Malua until I had a look inside. That might be invading Nakai's privacy, but I had been troubled since I had first met the Japanese. It might be contrary to my nature but if that box could help satisfy my curiosity, I could use that as my rationale for opening it. "I'll remind you, Sammy."

The supply shuttle from Viti Levu arrived on schedule and for the next few days, only Niko and Sarah shared the island with me. We reminisced about our time together and our adventures aboard the *Mary Margaret*. Niko gave the island generator a thorough checkup. It was housed in its own shelter, far enough inland that the noise of it running could seldom be heard. The long cable to the village showed no sign of deterioration and there was ample fuel for the next months. Niko also fished the lagoon and stocked the freezer with his cleaned catch.

The day came when I knew my crew was getting restless and they were just making work to justify their existence. I called them into the dining area. We sat for a last drink together.

I thanked them both with a toast and then pushed a thick, document-sized manila envelope across the table to Niko.

"Everything you need is here; I've included a year's salary plus a bonus that you both have certainly earned. I want you to take the *Mary Margaret* to Honolulu and sell her. Change her name first and re-register her." I grinned. "Mary Margaret stays here with me.

"Contact Miki Cavanaugh; she's a yacht broker that will get us a good deal. Her card is in the envelope and I've already talked to her. She will keep fifteen percent of the proceeds. Each of you is to receive another fifteen percent. The rest goes to the Kamehameha Schools for native Hawaiians."

Sarah commented, "That's a generous donation, Mister Foster, to us as well as the school. We're going to miss you."

I could see the moisture in her eyes. "When you settle somewhere, send me your address. We have to keep in touch."

Niko nodded, obviously in the same emotional state as his wife.

I placed a hand on Niko's shoulder. "We shouldn't prolong this. I know you're anxious to sail." I also knew they had already stocked provisions and had their personal gear on board.

There was really no reason to stay another minute.

We stood and Sarah embraced me, kissing me on the cheek several times. She could no longer contain her tears. It was good to feel her young body pressed against me, her warmth the reflection of a young woman who knew she was like a daughter to me.

"Oh!" she exclaimed suddenly and ran behind the bar to immediately return with a lei of Vaka Malua's flowers. She placed it over my head with a final kiss. Then, she whispered a secret I had long wished to hear, "I'm pregnant; Niko doesn't know yet." Aloud, she added "We knew you were ready for us to go. Aloha, Captain."

Niko took his leave. "Captain, we will never again know and love such a man and woman. You will always be in our thoughts and we wish you good *mana* for the rest of your years."

I met the handsome Hawaiian's sincere hug with a warm embrace of my own. "Go. Get out of here. The tide's going out."

I escorted them down to the Zodiac and stood ankle deep in the lagoon as they motored out to the *Mary Margaret*. Too quickly, the Zodiac was hauled on board and secured. I watched and heard Sarah start the diesel. She gently eased the *Mary Margaret* ahead to take the strain off the anchor cable while Niko detached the keel line and engaged the windlass. Within minutes they passed out the channel through the reef. Sarah stood on the boom and waved vigorously back at me.

The mainsail rose and filled with a healthy wind. Niko steered the *Mary Margaret* on a starboard tack toward Viti Levu. I knew they would take on one or two young deckhands, most probably teenagers, for the long sail to Hawaii. What an adventure that would offer for a lucky pair of young men.

I watched the sloop with moisture-laden eyes until its sails were but a white-tipped dot on the blue horizon. Suddenly, I was aware of the immense silence on Vaka Malua. Except for a barely perceptible lapping of the lagoon upon the sand and just a whisper of the wind through the trees behind the village, there was nothing. Such silence only reigns in the absence of men, and only a man alone can hear it.

I was alone except for the ever-present sand crabs.

I wished I could see the expressions on Niko's and Sarah's faces as they opened the two white envelopes I had placed in the larger manila one. One was marked: 'Do not open until Vaka Malua is over the horizon'.

The first contained certified checks for their pay and bonuses plus $3,000 in cash. It would be more than ample to start them on their way and in the light of Sarah's whispered secret I was glad I had been generous.

The second note would be quite a shocker and I recalled the joy as I had written it:

"Dear Niko and Sarah,

I lied. The sloop is yours and the necessary signed and notarized documents are enclosed. I ask only one thing: please register her under the name
Pa'aloha...."

Pa'aloha; in English, means 'Keepsake'. Now they would always remember me. And I was amazed at my own clairvoyance, for on an impulse, I had added:

"The forward stateroom would make an excellent nursery. This is a gift of my love to you, my children, and it makes me very happy.

Aloha and mahalo,
Donald Foster"

I was sure that the note would prompt Sarah to reveal her secret to her husband. *Papa Niko!* I had to laugh. The expression had a lilting ring to it. I could hear it flowing off of Sarah's tongue as she told him of the baby.

I waded in the receding waters for several minutes. It felt good. At the moment, I was complete and satisfied. This could be a great time for me. I had so many things I wanted to read and the lounge had several racks of books, mostly paperbacks but many were of quality. I had always wanted to paint and I would gather up the necessary art supplies on my first visit to Viti Levu.

I needed to reestablish myself with my God. There was nothing left in life that I particularly wanted to accomplish. I knew there would be times when I would go over to Viti Levu for supplies, times when I felt I really needed human contact.

I had a real need to understand what my purpose on earth had been. Why, with all of the good that had happened to me, did I feel that something was lacking? I let one hand drop to my testicles. If only Mary Margaret and I could have produced children...

※　※　※

For some time, I walked the beach. I breathed the air, my air. An incredibly blue sky domed overhead. I pictured myself as Adam in the Garden of Eden. He had it little better. With a certain remorse, I remembered that the whole South Pacific had been like this, virtually untouched, certainly unspoiled, just a single lifetime back. Was present day living any better than that? When contrasted with the intense business world that I had lived in for a half-century, this was another planet. Within just my tenure on it, population growth, instant communications and jet travel had pulled the Earth into itself as if it were a black hole, sucking in even the energies of the people as they found themselves faced with the ever escalating demands of society.

I was indeed privileged for my world now extended only to the oceanic horizon around me.

I checked my watch. Why? My time should not have to be measured by some repetitive and inconsequential sixty-minute period. I slid the elastic band from my wrist and pitched the timepiece as far out into the lagoon as I could. The sun would remind me of my place in the overall scheme of things. I had all the time there was.

One thing I knew instinctively: it was not too early for a drink. Walking behind the bar, my eyes caught Nakai's green metal box where it sat back against the mirror and partially hidden by some glasses. I had deliberately put it there. I knew that Sammy would probably leave without it. I poured my drink, took the box and sat down on one of the bar stools. While I sipped the bourbon, I gazed at the box. What right did I have to open it? None. Yet the temptation overwhelmed me. It was as if there were some force inside me that insisted I do so. Perhaps, it really wouldn't be a bad thing, just impolite. If there was nothing unusual there, no harm would be done. But that green metal box represented some part of Nakai, and some part of him—his eyes!—had triggered an intense and irresistible curiosity in my own soul. I decided to defy my own best judgement.

As before, the box was locked, but didn't seem very secure. I leaned over the bar and grabbed a small screwdriver that was sometimes used to punch holes in the cans of tomato or orange juice. I began to try and pry it open, being careful to avoid excessive scratching or bending. After a few minutes of probing and twisting with the screwdriver, the top came loose.

Inside were all sorts of papers and I could see right away that they were all in Japanese. I scanned several of them, mostly old newspaper clippings of Nakai's business achievements. One had a fairly recent picture of him. I was surprised to learn that he had enjoyed a brief career in the Japanese Self-Defense Forces. A few of the contents were legal documents. A deed to his home on Hokkaido. A bill of sale for his business. There was a bundle of letters, most quite old. Near the bottom were some pictures, held together with a rubber band. I immediately recognized Nakai and two children, who were most probably his grandchildren. One was taken in front of the great Buddha at Kamakura. There were several severely weathered and worn photos of Nakai and his wife, she in the traditional wedding kimono and elaborate hair-do, he in an ill-fitting tuxedo. There was a commercial picture of Emperor Hirohito sitting arrogantly in the saddle of a white horse. A plastic wrap similar to Saranwrap® protected the picture. I stuck my tongue out at it.

Finally, there was a picture of a young soldier, a formal picture taken against a painted backdrop of Mount Fuji. I knew it must be Nakai but the man was so young. I moved down the bar where there was better light. Yes, it was Nakai, all right. I chuckled. It had to be a wartime picture, very similar to the stiffly posed photos many of us had made as we went off to fight for our homeland. It had probably sat in his parent's house during those difficult years.

I tilted the box to see if there was anything else. Stuck to the bottom was some kind of card, wallet-sized and encased in a sealed plastic bag. Even before I could open it, I could tell that it was an identification card and when I pulled it clear, I could see a full-face head shot of Nakai in the upper left corner. Surprisingly, at the top of the card were the English words: 'Allied Occupation Forces, Japan'. Below was a short paragraph in Japanese followed by the English translation: 'This identification card will be kept on your person at all

60

times and will be shown to allied authorities upon request.' There was a final line: 'ID#352665, Japanese national: Hanaki Mishataka'. The card was authenticated by a Major Philip Moore, U.S. Army, Provost Marshall, Yokohama Military District, Allied Forces.

I stood transfixed. The impossible had happened! It simply could not be! Suddenly, my ears could not hear, my nose could not smell, and my mouth could not taste. Only my eyes functioned, and even they had no peripheral vision. Everything except my direct view of the name, Hanaki Mishataka, was blocked out. It was as if I had walked through an open door from one world to another.

On one side of the door, the side from whence I had come, there had been a gentle man named Donald Foster, a retired businessman and sailor, a man who had enjoyed a long life with a wonderful woman.

On this side of the door, where I was now, there was a much younger man, an angry, vengeful man who had suddenly been reawakened by an impossible circumstance. The rage that had surfaced with my realization that I was at this moment only a few miles away from my lifelong demon was all consuming and oblivious to any other emotion I might feel.

I had never prayed for this opportunity; it had been such an improbability.

Feeling as if I was having an out-of-body experience, I stared, transfixed, at the picture of the young Nakai in his army uniform. He was wearing sergeant's insignia. I looked back at the identification card.

Sweet Jesus!

Nakai was not Nakai. Somewhere along the line he had

61

changed his name and I knew why.

I sank to my knees as a debilitating mental image exploded in my head, so intense I felt my skull would split. On this side of the door, it was suddenly early August, 1945. I was a naked, emaciated 17-year old U.S. Marine in a Japanese prison camp south of Yokohama, kneeling on urine-soaked dirt in the noonday sun. My eyes swollen shut from an early morning beating, my dry lips cracked and bleeding, my swollen tongue almost cutting off my air supply, my soul crying out for the mercy of death.

Sergeant Hanaki Mishataka, Imperial Army of Japan, was lashing my back with a leather whip. He had done so, twice a day, for the last seventy-three days.

CHAPTER 5

THE PLAN

I had no idea how long I had been on the floor, reliving the most terrible memories of my life. They surged back into my consciousness in great detail from the time I had lied about my age and enlisted in the Marines. It had been November, 1944, and I found myself caught up in the super-patriotism that permeated every U.S. male, especially underage teenagers whose hormones had them teetering on the brink of manhood. My actual age was only sixteen. But I was big and strong and the Marines didn't ask a lot of questions. I had an altered birth certificate and my mother's forged permission.

The memories raced across the screen of my mind, each overlapping the other. I recalled in vivid detail the unbelievably harsh boot camp at San Diego where God-like, combat-hardened DIs molded me into an embryonic Marine in six weeks. I enjoyed liberty, beer and prostitutes in Tijuana while I waited to ship out. I revisited the excitement of my first boat trip, the passage to Hawaii, as foreign a land as China to me in those days. I recollected the hard days of replacement training on Oahu and then the long voyage in the unbelievably crowded troop transport to join the 1st Marine Division on the final assault of the war, the invasion of Okinawa, April 1, 1945, Easter Sunday. It was the first Easter that I had not gone to Mass. It had also been April Fool's Day.

Finally, I relived the descent down the thick-roped nets

into the bobbing LCVPs, my heart racing and mouth very, very dry. We beached, the big flat bow plate dropped and I was running as fast as I could through knee-deep water, my rifle held high over my head, knowing for sure that the next moment would be my last on Earth.

To our amazement, the landings had been unopposed. It was a welcome surprise. We did not then know that it was part of the Japanese strategy. They allowed us to penetrate deep into the island to where we no longer had fire support of naval units. Then the Nips struck back in a vicious ambush. On the first day of actual combat, I did become a man. I yelled and I killed and I vomited and I dirtied myself with diarrhea and I wallowed, overcome with hate and fear. I learned that the DIs in boot camp had been exactly right. My best friend in the world *was* my rifle and the next best was the Marine closest to me.

During the engagement, a nearby exploding artillery round knocked me cold. It produced a concussion and minor flesh wounds. When I came to, it was dusk and Japanese soldiers were dragging me across an isolated beach. They placed me in a small boat with three other American prisoners. For some inexplicable reason, we were taken to Japan on the last submarine to escape from the waters around Okinawa.

After a series of beatings and interrogations in small transient holding camps, I eventually wound up at a main POW camp south of Yokohama. It was primarily for American prisoners who were to be executed as soon as the first allied soldier set foot on the home islands of Japan. The Japanese knew they had lost the war but were prepared for mass slaughter and a fight-to-the-last-man effort when the time came.

It was at the camp that I was taken under the personal care

of Sergeant Hanaki Mishataka, a brutal man who was only a couple years older than I. His stocky build, shaved head, and wire glasses were burned into my memory like a brand. I had never known that a human being could be so merciless and the unrestrained hate that glinted in Mishataka's eyes completely eclipsed my own.

Now, fifty-three years later, the beast was only thirty-two miles away on the island of Viti Levu. Never, in all of the five decades, had I ever expected to come across my tormentor again.

My first impulse was to go over to Viti Levu and simply beat the bastard to death, but the Japanese might be the stronger even if several years older. Both of us were old men and a direct confrontation might not be the best way to go. Besides, that would be too obvious an action and I would wind up a criminal. No, I needed a plan, one that would place Mishataka under my absolute control. Then, I would beat the shit out of him.

Even as I thanked God for such fortune, I knew that I would be risking my very soul for what I was about to do. I was surprised at the naked cruelty of my own thoughts. That was not like me, but it had been another world when I first encountered Mishataka. Now, that world had returned. The good days were gone.

I picked myself up from the floor. It was dark and I was weak from the shock of the reentry of Mishataka into my life. I had much to do but it would have to wait until morning. Meanwhile, I could drink myself to sleep. It took a while; second thoughts prompted me to go easy on the bourbon.

At one point, I think I entered the nether world that dwells deep within us all, the place where we go when circumstances

65

overpower us and shut off our reasoning and understanding. I remember pounding my fists on the floor until my knuckles were blood red. There must still be present within some hidden corner of our brains a vestige of our primal selves that governs emotion when we struggled to walk on two limbs a million or so years back. I had an animal urge to kill.

I must have screamed Mishataka's name a thousand times into the night. How I gathered myself together, I may never know. But, after a while, I did. My reasoning returned, motivated by the realization that I would have to keep my wits about me to think this opportunity through. Finally, totally exhausted, I slept for several hours, all in the company of Sergeant Mishataka and his leather whip.

I foraged around the staff hut and found several machetes. Sammy's was the sharpest of the lot and I used it to cut down a large pile of bamboo stalks. All were approximately two inches in diameter and varied in length from three to five feet. I brought strong nylon cord from the storeroom and I used it to lash together the two structures I would need. Both would be on the north side of the island near the bamboo grove and the crater rim. The first would be a lean-to.

The frame went up quickly. I anchored it firmly in the sand, cross-driving pointed bamboo stakes as deeply as I could. I would not be able to climb the coconut trees so I had to make do with old palm fronds that had fallen off. They would be less water resistant, so I placed several layers on the lean-to to compensate.

On the second day, I stocked the structure with duct tape, a poncho, canned goods, a few eating utensils, and a pot for boiling rice. I filled several plastic jugs with drinking water and placed them in the shade of the bamboo stand. Finally, I gathered some driftwood.

The second structure took me the rest of the day and part of the next as it had to be one that would be impossible to dismantle. There was no need to anchor it; it was too heavy to blow away. I placed it where at high tide the water would just lap the bottom. I was going to do terrible things but I was not quite as inhumane as Mishataka had been. I didn't want the old man to die too soon and even in my rage, I was determined to maintain some sense of decency.

I gave the area a final inspection, made a few mental notes to bring over a couple items I had overlooked and smiled with satisfaction. It was hot on the beach. Without protection, over a period of several days, a man could literally cook to death.

Back at my village, I gathered anything that could be used as a hand weapon, placed the lot in a drawer, wrapped it in cloth and buried it behind the staff hut. I disabled the transmission capability of the radio, then hid the cellular telephone and the keyboard to the computer. I took my 9mm Glock semiautomatic from the plastic bag and inserted a full clip. I would never have had any use for it on the island but it had been kept on the *Mary Margaret* whenever we were at sea. Niko did not like guns and had brought it ashore with the rest of my things. I placed it in the waistband of my shorts and exchanged my T-shirt for a long aloha type garment.

I was satisfied. It was time to go to Viti Levu.

❇ ❇ ❇

My suite at the Fiji Hilton was available as usual and I took time to sit and go over what I must do. First, I must calm myself. My heart was racing and I was nervous. For the last forty-eight hours, I had been pushing myself. The next stage of my plan must be carried out more methodically. There was no room for mistakes.

After the dinner hour, I walked into the hotel lounge and sat at the bar. I had previously checked and as I had been informed, Nakai was on duty.

"Good Evening, Mister Foster. Good to see you again. How are things on Vaka Malua?"

"Fine, Nakai." It was difficult to be casual, even harder to be pleasant. "Just tonic with a little lime, please."

Nakai served me and left to take care of several other customers.

I watched his every move but was careful to divert my eyes if the Japanese looked my way. At one point, I had asked, "What time are you off?"

"My shift end early tonight. Ten o'clock."

"Maybe we could have a cup of coffee together. I'd like to tell you what I've accomplished in the last two days."

I could see that Nakai was a bit embarrassed by the invitation. He probably did not consider himself on the same social level as his former employer but I knew that he would consider it impolite to refuse. He answered with a counter proposal, "I only live short distance. I would be honored to have you as guest. I have excellent *sake* and I usually prepare light dinner after work."

That will be even better, I thought. "Thank you. I would enjoy that."

As we left the hotel, I tried to calm my adrenaline rush. I felt light-headed yet confident in my ability to do what I knew had to be done. It was just a matter of self- control.

Nakai's apartment was, indeed, only a five-minute walk away, a small second-floor studio type with a front window that overlooked the harbor.

"This is very nice," I commented, following Nakai's lead by leaving my shoes outside the door and accepting the offered cloth slippers.

"Thank you. It is suitable for my needs."

The place was furnished in traditional Japanese style. Tatami mats were on the floor and on them sat a low wooden table and a scattering of cushions. A red cloisonné vase, holding one white flower and a sprig of greenery sat on the table. A large blue futon was rolled and stowed upright in one corner. A two-burner propane hot plate sat on a simple but elegantly built white wood support. It was waist high and a small cabinet, also of the same material, sat beside it. On the other side was an older refrigerator.

A three-panel, silk screen divider was arranged in another corner and on it was a watercolor painting of a large white crane in flight.

Nakai placed a small black lacquered bowl of oriental snacks on the table. I folded my legs beneath me in order to sit on one of the larger cushions. My leg muscles cried out in anguish at the unfamiliar position and I had to adjust my posture as the barrel of the Glock dug into my groin.

After warming the sake on the hot plate, Nakai served it from a six-inch tall white porcelain bottle. He filled two sake cups to the brim and handed one to me with a deep bow. "You honor my home."

"Kanpai," I toasted. Cheers.

We drank together and I poured the next round.

"You have been very busy, *hai*?" Nakai asked.

"Kanpai," I answered, raising my cup.

We drank together and Nakai poured the next round.

I quickly raised my cup. *"Kanpai."*

The pace was too fast for Nakai. He downed his warm rice wine, then stood before I could pour another.

"I have something for us," he said. "Excuse me for moment." He bowed and made himself busy at the hot-plate, taking several items from the refrigerator and preparing them while we talked.

"I have been busy at Vaka Malua. I'm looking forward to showing you what I've done," I commented. "I think you will be surprised."

"Did Niko and Sarah depart?"

"Oh, yes, they sailed several days back."

There was a chopping noise, followed by the sizzle of oil and vegetables, then the odor of fresh fish and finally an appetizing aroma of the final mixture. Nakai served the meal on a pair of exquisite white Noritaki plates, the vegetables and fish arranged over and around a ball of soft white rice. He had garnished each plate with a red turnip rose.

We ate in silence for only a moment.

"You mentioned once that you were in the army during the war," I ventured.

Nakai was not quick to answer and when he did it was a simple, "Yes."

"Where were you stationed?" As I asked, I filled the sake cups. *"Kanpai."*

"Kanpai." Nakai only sipped his cup. "May I serve you more?" he asked, motioning with his head toward the food.

"No, this is superb. You were saying?"

"I was assigned mostly to training duties. Southern Kyushu and later on, Tokyo area. I was very young."

You lying bastard.

"I was, too. A boy marine, actually, but I was big for my age."

Nakai raised his cup. "You marines were good warriors. In our army, it was great honor to go against you. We Japanese always had great respect for samurai tradition, soldiers willing to die for their country. U.S. Marines, I think, were like samurai."

"I'm afraid not. We didn't go into battle to die for our country; we went into battle to make some other bastard die for his country."

I could see that Nakai was uncomfortable with the harshness in my voice. He straightened his back. "Those times are long past."

"For some."

He bowed, then continued, "Yes, I imagine it is difficult for many soldiers to put war behind them. Our generation was caught up in great tragedy." It appeared that Nakai wanted to make a point to me but he was unsure as how to go about it. I could read him like a book. In traditional Japanese fashion, he did not want to appear antagonistic but he did not want me to feel he was ashamed of his service. In fact, he sounded quite determined. "I think all soldiers alike. We fought for country. We did our duty. We obey orders." He looked me squarely in the eyes. "In those days, you and I were very much alike. I think we should erase any bad memories and recall pride as soldiers. Only the politicians should live in shame."

I could agree with him on that one. I poured more *sake* and toasted, *"Kanpai."* Nakai downed his in one gulp. I sat mine on the table.

"We were not exactly alike, Nakai. You say you stayed in Japan. I got my ass waxed on Okinawa."

Nakai stiffened even further. He knew that I was deliberately trying to pick an argument with him. I sensed it was not an argument he wished to engage in; it was not an argument either of us could win. I suspected that he did not wish to be inhospitable but talking about events that happened more than fifty years ago, with the degree of emotion that I was beginning to show, could in no way be constructive.

"Forgive me, Mister Foster, but my day very long and I am sure you share need for rest. I suspect your tomorrow will start early as mine." Nakai started to stand.

"Not yet," I declared. My eyes burned into his. In my right hand I held the Glock, its barrel pointed at his chest.

Nakai did not allow himself to panic although at that particular moment he must have had the distinct feeling that I was going to kill him. He could not know the reason for my sudden change of attitude. Forcing himself to speak slowly and evenly, he asked, "Mister Foster, what are you doing? Have I angered you some way? Is it because of the war? It has been more than half-century."

"I can't count it in that broad a term. For me, it has been days, thousands and thousands of days. And it was a rare one among them during which I did not curse you."

"Curse *me*? I personally did you no harm. We did not meet in combat. We were victims of times." Anger was replacing

Nakai's initial fright and confusion.

"You don't have the slightest idea who I am, do you?"

Nakai shook his head. He probably figured that he was in the presence of a madman.

"Well, *Sergeant Hanaki Mishataka*, I know you."

He gasped as if hit in the chest with a two-by-four. "You are crazy. *Bakatada!*"

"No! I'm not crazy. I'm just a piece of flesh wrapped around fifty-three years of hate. And you, Sergeant Mishataka, are a god-damned war criminal who almost got away."

"You are mistaken." He had regained his composure. "I am Mirata Nakai. I never heard of Sergeant Mishataka."

"How about POW Camp Twelve, south of Yokohama?"

"I was teaching soldier. Never station Yokohama." Nakai's English was beginning to break down.

"South of Yokohama, *Sergeant*."

"Never."

"I have proof."

"Impossible."

My hand tightened on the Glock. With my other hand, I yanked back the slide and cocked the semi-automatic. It would only take the slightest loss of control for me to kill the Japanese, here and now, murder charge be damned. "Get up. We're going for a boat ride."

Nakai stood. "I do not wish this. I will not go. I don't understand what you are doing. Are we going to Vaka Malua? I have no quarrel with you. You have mistaken me for someone else." He had stood but refused to budge. "Let me show you identification. I have birth record, army record, employment identification, official papers. Marriage certificate..."

"You don't have shit, sergeant. Everything you have is a lie. I have the real stuff. You left it behind, on the island, in the green box."

"You have no right to see my personal things."

I grabbed Nakai's arm just before we went outside. "We're going to walk down to the marina and take the boat very calmly and quietly. I want you to understand one thing. If you do anything, yell, try to run, fall down, any god-damned thing to attract attention, I will kill you. I don't care how many people are there, I will put a bullet into your spine with the greatest of pleasure."

Nakai jerked his arm away. "You cannot get away with that."

"That's right. But you will be dead and I will have achieved a goal in life that I never thought would come."

Nakai defiantly responded, "I have nothing to gain by letting you take me to your island. You will kill me there."

"You didn't kill me when you had your chance, Sergeant. I may return the favor. We'll talk about it. It's a big gamble for you, but the only one you have."

It was after midnight and we passed only a few late-nighters on the way to the marina. I did not want Nakai to have any doubts that I would kill him if he resisted. If he did, he might call what he perceived to be my bluff. So I intentionally shoved the Glock into his side several times as we walked.

We reached my boat slip. "Get in," I ordered. As Nakai stood in the cockpit, I reached in a stowage box and retrieved a roll of gray duct tape. "Hands behind you." I taped them firmly together.

"In the cabin. I've removed anything you could use as a weapon so sit down and enjoy the ride." I closed the hatch after him and latched it.

The moon was still bright and the seas calm as we raced toward Vaka Malua. The few persons we had encountered had shown no signs of suspicion and since none spoke, I assumed none knew Nakai.

I had committed my first felony; I was a kidnapper. It was an unpleasant thought but one which gave me little cause for concern. I did not want to dwell upon the consequences of what I was going to do. My mind was too occupied with the thoughts of how I was going to make Sergeant Mishataka regret his actions at POW Camp Twelve. Besides, the consequences were irrelevant when I considered the satisfaction. At last, I would be able to even the score. Maybe then, I could forget. I doubted that I would ever forgive.

I thanked the overhead moon for giving me the visibility I needed to pass through the reef and make our way around to north beach. There, I ran the eighteen-footer gently up onto the sand and killed the engine. I unlatched the cabin hatch. Nakai preceded me off the boat and stood transfixed. There, ahead of him was the lean-to, set back in the trees. But the structure that held his eyes and I knew caused him to have the first inklings of what could be in store for him was the second structure. It was a bamboo cage.

I had built a three- by four- by two-foot wide structure. The longitudinal end poles and the vertical side poles were spaced only three inches apart. The cage was held together by multiple lashings at every intersection of bamboo. The near end was open, the hatch hinged and folded back to the left.

"Welcome to POW Camp Twelve, Sergeant Mishataka." I prodded the Japanese with my Glock and had him pause before the cage. I stood behind him as I cut loose the duct tape. "Strip," I ordered.

"What?"

"Strip!"

"What are you going to do?" Nakai asked. A slight tremor edged his voice despite his attempt to speak calmly.

I reached inside the cage and pulled out a narrow length of torn white sheet while Nakai undressed.

"You make your own loincloth, Sergeant. It's all you'll need here."

"Mister Foster. It is not too late. *Doso*, we talk about this."

"From now on, it's Corporal Foster, US Marine Corps. We'll talk after you're in the cage."

Nakai wrapped the folded strip around his waist, drew one end down the crack of his buttocks and between his legs, then up and under the waistband where he secured it with the other end across his stomach.

"The cage!" I ordered.

Nakai stooped and entered the cage. He could neither stand erect nor lie down fully so he half-sat in the far corner as I secured the entry with a short reach of chain and lock. I knew that at the moment he would look upon the cage as a terrible thing but he would get to love it as I did, for when I was in the cage, no matter how sore and cramped I was, I could not be beaten. I had come to look upon my cage as a refuge and I was determined that the Japanese would know that feeling.

I waved the Glock as I spoke, "If I catch you trying to get out, I'll kill you. Remember, at this point, I'm really looking for an excuse to do just that."

"You said talk."

"Go ahead."

"Why you doing this?"

I placed the Glock in a ziplock bag and stuck it my waist-band.

"I've already told you. You're a war criminal who committed atrocities against allied personnel, namely me, during the period of June through August 1945. After the occupation, you deliberately falsified your identification to escape justice. You are here while I deliberate with myself on two possibilities. One, I can now call the authorities and have them come over and pick you up and I'll be a star witness at your trial."

"And the other?"

"I will beat the shit out of you and then call the authorities. That's really my more attractive option."

"I am not Hanaki Mishataka."

I walked over to the lean-to and brought back the green metal box. "Who is this?" I asked, holding up the picture of Nakia with the two children.

"That is private property! You have no right to open."

"Who is this?"

"That is me. My grandchildren."

"I never had grandchildren, Sergeant. I never had children. How about this?" I held up the wedding picture.

"That is brother and wife."

"Brother? That's a fucking lie if ever I heard one! I suppose this is your brother's occupational ID card?"

"Yes."

"Then, your brother was Sergeant Hanaki Mishataka? What kind of bullshit is that?"

"I was adopted."

I banged the cage with my fist. "Listen, you son of a bitch, don't play games with me. This is fucking *you*!"

"No. Brother."

I stuck my face as closely as I could toward his, "You say that one more time and I'm going to set this cage on fire and send you straight to hell. This is *your* ID."

Nakai seemed now to have complete control of himself. "If I am prisoner of war then Geneva Convention applies. I give only name, rank and serial number. I am thirsty. Give drink, please."

"Give me your name, rank and serial number."

"Mirata Nakai, sergeant, Imperial Japanese Army, 13323491."

"Wrong answer."

"My water, please."

I'll give you water. I walked over to the lean-to and brought back a half-coconut shell. I proceeded to the edge of the lagoon, filled it and passed it into the cage through one of the gaps in the horizontal end bars.

"I cannot drink sea water."

"Your name!"

"Mirata Nakai."

"Tell you what, Mirata Nakai. You sleep on it." I walked over to the lean-to, picked up one of the water jugs and took a long swig, swirled the precious liquid inside my mouth and spat it out onto the sand. Then, I laid down and closed my eyes. "Get some sleep, Sergeant," I called out. "We've got a full day, tomorrow."

❊   ❊   ❊

I awoke at first light. Nakai was sitting cross-legged in the cage, his shoulders forward and head bowed but still pressed against the top of the cage. He showed no signs of being awake but I doubted it was a sound sleep, more likely a semi-sleep state caused by fatigue and cramps. Good.

I started a fire, put a pot half-filled with water on it and dumped in several hands full of rice. I walked over to the cage and began urinating on Nakai.

"Ayeeeeeeee!" Nakai jerked and squirmed as he realized what was happening. His eyes flashed with rage then went stone cold.

"Wake up, sergeant."

"Stop! You are mad!" Nakai lapsed into Japanese and I knew he was cursing me.

I shook the remaining droplets onto his legs. "Bring back memories, Sergeant Mishataka? You pissed on me at least once a day every day for seventy-three fucking days. Remember how I heaved my guts out the first few times? A brave samurai like you, pissing on a helpless seventeen-year old boy."

Nakai yelled, "This is not true! You are beast!" He groaned as his sudden movements caused bursts of pain to travel through stiff joints and cramped muscles. Furious, he shook the cage. "Let me out! You cannot do this!"

I replied, "That's where you're wrong. I can do any god-damned thing I want!"

"This is madness. I will die here. You will kill me, Foster."

"Corporal Foster, United States Marine Corps."

"You have not been a Marine for last half-century. Marines are honorable warriors. This is not honorable thing to do. The war is over, Foster."

I jerked my Glock from my waist, stripped off the plastic bag and fired two quick shots into the cage, aiming such that the rounds barely missed the Japanese. "Corporal Foster, United States Marine Corps. *My* war is not over. Nor yours." I wanted to jerk the Japanese from the cage and beat him until he admitted he was Sergeant Mishataka. Then, I would beat him for *being* Sergeant Mishataka. But the man had not been in the cage long enough. He was still stubborn. In fact, the more I harassed him, the more likely would be his resistance. Deep inside my soul there lingered the instinct of a fighting Marine who had been horribly abused; likewise, there was reason to believe that deep in the soul of the Japanese, the code of *bushido* was still present. Maybe, all I was accomplishing was bringing it out.

It was getting hot. I walked over to the water jug and drank. The Japanese did not even look at me. But I knew what he was feeling. His lips would be dry and his tongue occasionally sticking to the roof of his mouth. But there was still saliva and Nakai could wet his lips. He had to be weak after a night in the cage. It wouldn't be too much longer before he would be unable to even swallow for there would be nothing there. At that point, his throat would begin to dry out and swell and his tongue would lose all taste.

The water in the rice pot was boiling and I stirred it with a stick. I would let it boil until the rice became a sticky white mass. Meanwhile, I would let the rising sun take over the interrogation.

❈ ❈ ❈

By noon, the rice was done. I scooped out a bowl full. Nakai watched. His body was covered with the life-giving fluid that should have remained within it. His mouth was dry and he could not close it. There would be moisture in the white grain.

Turning my back to my captive, I added a small amount of sand and several grubs I had gathered for the purpose. I stirred the mixture, walked over and offered it to Nakai.

The Japanese eagerly grabbed it; using two fingers, he threw a large portion into his mouth. So thirsty was he, he tasted the first sweet flavor of moisture and immediately gulped down the food. He chewed the second mouthful, and immediately spat it out. Not only had he bitten into the gritty sand, he had half-eaten several grubs and the bittersweet mucus taste made him gag. There was insufficient moisture in his system to vomit. He glared at me. "This, monkey shit. I will starve first."

I inwardly smiled at Nakai's inadvertent first use of language associated with POW Camp Twelve. The allied captives there had coined the term 'monkey shit' for the slop fed them.

"You'll get used to it. I did. After a while, I recognized that the dirt —you gave me dirt, I give you sand —kept my intestines irritated and working and the bugs and insects were a valuable source of protein. I lived on it. So can you."

"I not eat monkey shit!"

"Hell, your goddamned combat rations were practically the same thing. You waged military campaigns on such garbage. I lived on it, and much worse, for seventy-three days. You'll eat it or starve."

"What must I do to end this?"

"You can start by admitting who you are."

He shook his head in exasperation. I could see that he was

weighing the pros and cons of such an admission. To continue to refuse would result undoubtedly in continued torture and within only a few days, he would be helpless. All hope of escape would be gone. He could not want me to take him to that point.

Nakai spit out his confession, "All right! I am Sergeant Hanaki Mishataka! You let me out, now."

I dropped to the sand beside the cage. "That's better. Now I have your attention. Sergeant Mishataka, you should be proud of me. This cage is almost an exact replica of the one you forced me to exist in. I built it well, yes? I even sat in it a few minutes after it was finished to see if it has the same feeling. And it comes close. Of course, you did let me out from time to time —to beat me, to taunt me with water and food. Now, I am going to return the favor. Beating for beating, filth for filth, despair for despair. But I will not do to you anything you did not do to me. That's fair, yes? Only, I can't do it for seventy-three days. That's a shame, but old men like us have to pace ourselves, right? Seventy-three days in this sun and you'll be dead. I won't allow that to happen —unless you beg me to. That's a possibility."

Mishataka tried to take a defiant posture but the cage would not allow it. "We are no longer at war, you and me. It was different back then. We did what was expected. We follow orders. I do not remember you."

"You will."

"Let me out!" Mishataka screamed as I walked away. There were things I must do. It was near high tide and the eighteen-footer was almost afloat. It still took considerable effort to push it into the lagoon and climb on board but I managed.

Mishataka cried out, "I must have water! *Skoshi misu, kudasai. Doso, Foster-san!"* Please, Mister Foster, give me a little water.

I made sure Mishataka could read my lips as I mouthed, "Fuck you, Sergeant." The engine caught. I spun the rudder wheel and aimed the eighteen-footer around the east end of the island.

The wind revitalized me. There was great satisfaction in torturing the Jap —my mind had reverted to the World War II terminology. I laughed at how politically incorrect I was being. Fuck political correctness. That creature in my cage was a fucking Jap sergeant who was going to pay for every single atrocity he had ever visited on a young, terror-stricken, pleading Marine. I let one hand drop to my testicles. And the best I would save for last.

CHAPTER 6

THE TORTURE

I gathered the two canoes, threw in the paddleboards and tethered the lot to the outrigger canoe. The eighteen-footer started on the first crank and I eased it over to where I could use the boat hook and tie the canoes to the stern. The run across the lagoon and out into open sea took only a few minutes and after casting them adrift I sped back through the entrance channel and made the slip in the boat house. I removed the battery from the eighteen-footer and with considerable effort carried it into the brush at the edge of the beach. There I placed it where it could not readily be found.

My timing had been excellent, for the supply shuttle from Viti Levu arrived within the hour. I met the boat as it beached its bow on the sand. One of the Fijian deck hands offloaded several boxes, mostly non-perishables.

"Where you want these, Mister Foster?" one of them asked.

"In the dining room would be fine."

I took several smaller boxes and the smattering of mail myself.

"That looks like it."

"*Vinaka,* Toko" I said, thanking the man.

"No problem. How it goin', Mister Foster?"

"Fine so far."

"You have some communications problems? We try to call you all day to see if you needed anything else."

"No, Toko. I have been moving some things around and haven't hooked everything back up yet."

"Okay. Give us a call. See ya next week."

I waved as the shallow draft boat backed off the sand. After stowing the supplies, I began the trek back to north beach. No need to take the eighteen-footer; the trail across the island was only a mile or so. I enjoyed the walk. Things were going well. It was mid-afternoon by the time I arrived.

Nakai sat oriental style in the cage, his shoulders hunched. He had removed his loincloth and evidence of a bowel movement dirtied one corner of the cage. Most of the feces had dropped through the bottom bars but enough had caught on the bamboo to render the space unusable. High tide had been earlier in the morning, so little had been washed away. The loincloth was draped over one of the top bars.

Mishataka glared at me. He knew the negligence was deliberate. "I need to clean the cage," he declared.

"High tide comes again in the morning. That'll wash it off. You're fortunate. There was no high tide in POW Camp Twelve. You made me squat in my own filth for weeks. The only thing I had to clean myself with was my hand. It got so bad, it caked on my buttocks and I had to wait for the sun to dry it before I could peel it off. You remember that, Sergeant? Only when the stench got too bad for *you* did you allow me to wash and then it was in water used by everybody else for the same purpose. You sit in your own stink for a while."

Mishataka remained silent for several minutes. Then, he asked, "You are Christian?"

"I try to be. At the moment, I don't feel I have any Christ-like qualities. They're on hold for the duration of our relationship."

"You have prayer that you say."

"We have many prayers. I haven't said them lately. I have other things on my mind."

"You have prayer that asks your God to forgive you as you forgive others."

"You know the Lord's Prayer?"

"I know of it. In ancient Shinto, we have similar thought, but our *kami*—our gods—are different. The concept of a Christian God is foreign to us but it seems like an admirable belief."

"So?"

"How does your prayer apply now? Are you asking your God to do to you what you do to me? If so, you must forgive me."

"I can't do that yet."

"Then, it would be bad thing if you die now, *hai*?"

"Are *you* going to kill me?" I asked.

"Maybe that will be." For the first time since he had been brought to my island, he smiled.

I did not intend to play mind games with Mishataka. "I'll answer to my God for anything I will do to you."

"How can you do that?"

I asked myself the same question. How could I do to the Japanese what I was doing without any qualms of conscience? I had none at the moment. The Jap sergeant deserved everything he was getting. I felt no remorse at all. There was a certain dislike for the filth I was forcing upon my captive but the man needed to know what it had been like. There was no other way.

Mishataka's voice had taken on a certain hoarseness. "I need water."

I walked over to the lean-to and retrieved one of the water jugs. I stood in front of Mishataka and drank heavily. "It's getting warm. I don't think you would enjoy warm water."

"*Doso.*"

I looked closely at Mishataka. He had a desperate thirst. That was obvious and I knew exactly how he felt. Even after fifty-three years, I could recall that dry-throated agony. It was perhaps the worst torture of all. I remembered my first drink of iced water after I got to the Tokyo hospital. I had been given water sooner than that but an Army nurse brought me that first taste of cold water. I started to gulp it but she gently held my hand. "Slowly," she had said, "just a half glass this time." Oh, God, how good it had been!

Now, that jug of water that I held just outside Mishataka's reach was the most important thing in the world to him. He would give anything in exchange, but he had nothing to give. He was pleading, but the proud bastard would not beg; not yet. So, the water could be held back a while longer. "Eat your rice. It is still moist."

The rice was dark with sand that had blown into the bowl, but there was some glisten to it. The grubs were certainly enjoying it. "Tell you what, Sergeant. I'll give you a fresh bowl."

I refilled it from the pot but didn't bother to throw in sand or insects. The rice was almost dry and it would only frustrate Mishataka as he tried to suck moisture from it. It would provide some sustenance but that was a necessary thing. I knew I had to keep the older Japanese from getting too weak. If that happened, what was to come would not register on the sergeant's numbed mind.

Mishataka tried to eat the rice and did manage to down

some of it. But it was having a reverse effect on his mouth. Instead of providing moisture, it absorbed what infinitesimal amount of saliva remained.

I took out my Glock. I undid the lock and pulled back the end of the cage. Mishataka's eyes became alive with anticipation. He was going to be allowed to stand, maybe even to wash! The feeling lasted only as long as it took him to painfully crawl out of the cage. By that time, I had picked up a length of one-half inch bamboo stalk and before the Japanese could manage to force his stiff and aching spine into an upright position, I whipped the bamboo across his shoulders. The blow carried such force that Mishataka pitched forward under it and landed face down in the hot sand. A red welt traced immediately across his back.

"Stand up, Sergeant" I ordered.

Mishataka knew this was insanity. But I, in turn, knew that he would not succumb to just one blow from the cane. If I wanted to whip him to death, I would have to overcome the spiritual strength of a samurai. With great effort, Mishataka stood.

Whissshpppppppp!

He had braced himself and he did not fall.

Whissshpppppppp!

He dropped to his knees. Anticipating the next blow, he tightened his stomach and back muscles and prepared to scream.

Whissshpppppppp!

"Aieeeeeeeeeeeee!" He forced his elbows back and made an extreme effort to rise from his knees. I hit him again with the cane, but he had entered the realm of *bushido* mind control. For the rest of the beating, he would feel nothing. His eyes were glazed and periodically his beaten body shook with a pronounced tremor.

Suffer, you bastard. Feel the pain I felt.

His breath came now in rapid shallow gulps and he was having difficulty keeping his head erect. Yet, there was a strange dignity that marked his pained demeanor. Somehow, he readied himself for the next blow. When it did not come, he seemed to sense that my hesitation came from a confused mind. I wanted him dead —but I did not wish to kill him.

Astonished, I watched him lean back on his knees. Then, with Herculean effort, he managed to stand. It took him a full minute to turn around and face me. It was a display of sheer will power that I could not have imagined.

"*Banzaiiiiiii!*" Mishataka shouted. He extended his arms and attempted to step toward me. Instead, he pitched forward, his head dropping between my feet. I raised the cane but could not swing it again. That was enough for now. Blood oozed from broken, split skin of the welts on Mishataka's back.

I had to drag the Japanese back into the cage.

※　※　※

For the rest of the afternoon, I sat in the shade of the lean-to and sucked on the jug of water. Mishataka remained in the position in which I had placed him.

Don't you die on me, you bastard, I thought. I knew Mishataka was seriously wounded and greatly weakened by the lack of water and food, but the old soldier should not be near death, not yet. I walked over and checked Mishataka's pulse and breath. The former was steady and strong; that meant a good heart. His breathing was labored and shallow. That was to be expected. I reached inside the cage and adjusted the

90

man's position to put less pressure on his lungs.

Mishatake moaned as I sprinkled water from the jug on the whipping cuts. There was no need to let them get infected. That could be a process that I could not stop once it began.

It was another hour before Mishataka recovered sufficiently to rearrange himself in the cage and gain some relief.

The first colors of sunset stained the bellies of the clouds as his blood had stained Mishataka's back. The sand crabs were emerging from their holes in the cooling sand and scurrying to the water's edge. It was feeding time. Mishataka watched them for a moment as if he were really interested. Perhaps he was, for he asked in a voice that seemed far away, "Are we really any better than these mindless creatures? They have only needs; no compassion, no understanding, no forgiveness. If they have no food, they will eat one another. Why don't you go ahead and kill me, Corporal Foster, United States Marine Corps?"

"It may come to that. But first, you will relive my worst days."

Mishataka's eyes seemed to go blank for a second. Then he spoke quietly, "The Americans will rape your women and eat your children."

"What did you say?"

Mishataka allowed himself a faint chuckle. "Our officers say you Americans would rape our women and eat our children. Especially Marines."

"You believed them?"

"Of course. Your propaganda posters had soldiers of Nippon with monkey faces and long tails. You were told we were less than human."

"An image enhanced by your rape of Nanking, the attack on Pearl Harbor, the Bataan death march, the San Tomas prison in Manila, the beheading of our POW pilots. Shall I go on? I also recall that you soldiers bragged that you would march in victory through central Tokyo wearing American scrotums as coin purses."

"No, that is ridiculous. And our attack on Pearl Harbor was legitimate act of declared war. Surprise is an honorable tactic."

"And a damned efficient one, especially if the victims did not know a war was on."

"We struck only military targets. Our goal was military defeat, not mass destruction of innocents. Was that worse than firebombing Tokyo? How do you judge your actions at Hiroshima and Nagasaki?"

"We're not going to get into that argument, Sergeant. Your war and mine were at POW Camp Twelve. It was personal. *Very* personal. I swore that I would kill you if we ever met again."

"Then why you delay satisfaction?"

"Because we have some reconciling to do. Some resolution of our two lives."

Mishataka sat silent. I could see that even the strain of a prolonged discussion was getting to be too much for him. What a shame we had not met earlier when both of us were still capable of a good one-on-one encounter. I would have felt much better about what I was doing.

Mishataka had beaten me twice a day at POW Camp Twelve. I cursed the fact that once a day was all the older Japanese could take. The bamboo had felt good in my hand and the smack of it across Mishataka's back had given me a sense of satisfaction that I had longed for over the past half-century.

Could it be that my God had answered my prayers? Would the Christian God present a lukewarm worshiper with such a chance to feel the exhilaration of revenge? That didn't seem right. God was not vengeful but He did administer justice, many times in mysterious ways. I wanted to believe that such was the rationale for my actions, but I exhaled deeply in recognition of the truth. I was not about God's work. I was about my own.

Not that I intended to reverse any of my decisions. Justice would be served even if it were only human justice. Contrary to my usual self, I would be patient. I would beat Sergeant Mishataka as often as I could, knowing that I could never repay him lash for lash. I would starve the Japanese to the point of crisis and deny him water to the point of complete dehydration. Then, I would give a little rice and a bit of water to rejuvenate the son of a bitch to the point where he could be beaten again. That was my preconceived plan and I loved it.

❉ ❉ ❉

When I awoke the next morning, I immediately smelled and saw the signs of dysentery. I had not expected it to come on so soon but age was the unknown factor. In any case, I had to restore Mishataka's system to more of a balance.

I opened the cage and motioned for Mishataka to come out. The Japanese could not.

"You're not going to stay in there and die on me, Sergeant," I declared. I allowed Mishataka to sip from the water jug. The old soldier nodded in gratitude as I touched his head. The skin was hot with fever. "Damn!"

I pulled Mishataka from the cage. There was nothing to fear, physically. I walked my captive over to the lagoon and made him wade out to where the water was hip-high. Then, I sat him down. "Wash yourself. You can have more water when you get out."

Mishataka nodded and began to slosh the water over his shoulders. It immediately gave him enough strength to sit unassisted. I used an empty jug to fetch water from the lagoon and clean the cage. I would let it get soiled again but for the moment I needed to keep my captive alive. As much as it galled me to realize it, I would have to give water to Mishataka or the dehydration would rapidly kill him.

I turned to check on the Japanese and my heart skipped a beat. Mishataka was gone! No, no, there he was, half-walking and half-swimming toward the deeper water of the lagoon. "Mishataka! Come back! Don't you dare! Get your ass back here, Sergeant!"

Mishataka reached deep water and began a valiant effort to swim away. Whether he was trying to escape or drown himself was a moot question. He was no longer under my physical control.

I grabbed my Glock and cooked off two rounds, close enough to splash water in Mishataka's face. The Japanese kept throwing his arms ahead of him in a continuing effort to get away from me. He floundered and sank for a moment, surfaced and vomited seawater.

"Shit!" I exclaimed. I put away my weapon and trotted into the water. Within a couple yards, I pulled to a strong overhead stroke and rapidly closed on Mishataka. We were about forty yards offshore when I reached him. It was as if I had grabbed a small crocodile! With unbelievable fury, he rolled and twisted and flailed at my face with his fists. One foot caught me in the groin but the drag of the water weakened its punch. I pulled him under and held him between my legs, intent on keeping him there until he quit struggling but he wiggled free and shot to the surface.

Thank God, in the water, I had a definite advantage. I grabbed a fistful of his hair, jerked his head back, slapped his face and spun him over on his back, wrapping his chin in an elbow carry. Mishataka continued to twist and squirm but he was definitely spent. "Let me die," he pleaded.

I was incensed that the man had almost snookered me. "If you die, fucker, it'll be because I killed you." I shook my free fist in front of his face.

Mishataka was limp by the time I hauled him out of the water. I gave the semiconscious Japanese several full swallows of the water from the jug. Then I forced him into a kneeling position and made him lean on the cage.

I was truly pissed. Despite the possibility of lethal damage, I laid the bamboo cane across Mishataka's back two more times and pushed him into the cage. I was disappointed that he had repaid my kindness with an effort to escape. "Only two fucking days, Sergeant, have we been at this. God, I wish we were younger. You try that again, and we end it, but it won't be quick, and it won't be pretty. I have a plan for you and we stick to the plan."

Mishataka was curled in a corner of the cage and bent into an impossible position. He was shaking and clenching his fists. I knew that deep down in his soul he had a reserve of power that he could use to challenge me if only the opportunity could be created. Then, I would have to kill him. He would make sure of that.

Sunset was complete. I could hear Mishataka cursing himself aloud for not delaying his effort. In the dark, I could have lost him and he could have made his way far out into the lagoon, so far that he would have had no energy left. There, he would have drowned.

❋ ❋ ❋

The next two days were trials for both Mishataka and me. I did not want to weaken the Japanese further but I did want his life to be miserable. I accomplished that in two ways. First, I did give him rice and water. Second, I refused to let him out of the cage and it was soon contaminated with more of his body waste. The hot sun was tanning Mishataka's naturally brown skin to a level where it was beginning to burn. The net result would be peeling and the formation of an extremely sensitive layer that would produce pain whenever it was stretched. While Mishataka's strength did improve, he found himself more immobile because of the stiffness of his joints and the tightness of his skin. From my viewpoint, it was not an unfavorable combination.

On the third day, I let the Japanese out to wash in the lagoon and stood by while he cleaned the cage. The price for that bit of freedom was a back lashing, three strokes of a fresh bamboo stalk that forced him to curse me and crawl back into the bamboo enclosure where he sat panting from the pain of the lashing and pleading for fresh water. I allowed him four ounces.

I decided that now was the time to reveal to Mishataka the prime reason for my hatred of him. Over the years, I could have forgiven the beatings and deprivation of food and water.

I could not forgive him for the ultimate irreversible damage he had made me suffer every day since August 15, 1945.

Mishataka watched me drop my shorts and underwear. He had no idea of what was coming next. For all of the abuse he may have heaped upon me at POW Camp Twelve, there had never been any sexual connotation. He became even more alarmed when I stood next to the cage.

"Grab my balls," I ordered.

"What?"

"My testicles, Sergeant. Grab my testicles."

Mishataka looked up at me and recoiled. "I will not do that."

"Yes, you will. Do it now and save yourself some pain."

Mishataka could see the determination in my eyes. It would serve no purpose for him to refuse further. Obviously, it was not a sexual invitation. I had no erection, not even any turgidity. He reached one arm through the bars and after a moment's hesitation cupped his hand around my scrotum.

"Squeeze," I directed.

Mishataka tightened his grip.

"Goddammit, I said 'squeeze'! Hard!"

I could see that he was very offended and uncomfortable, but he grasped as hard as he could. Perhaps, he thought it was an opportunity to return some of the pain that had been suffered upon him.

I just laughed. "Now, let go."

He did so immediately. He had gotten no satisfaction from the weird request.

"Notice anything?" I asked.

Mishataka shook his head.

"No pain, Sergeant Fuckhead. I felt no pain. You know

why? I don't have any balls. What you felt are silicone implants. Cosmetic testicles so that when I'm disrobed in front of other men, they have no idea I'm a eunuch." While I spoke, I picked up the bamboo cane. Now, I began to furiously pound the cage. Mishataka huddled on the far side. I moved over to his area, still pounding the cane. He squirmed away once more.

I had the Glock in my other hand. "Spread your legs."

Mishataka did not move. He obviously figured that if I intended to maim him, he would not help by giving me an easy shot.

I desperately wanted to pull the trigger but before I did, I wanted the Japanese to know exactly why. "You know why I have silicone balls, sergeant? Because on that last morning, only hours before your emperor came on the radio and announced that Japan had unconditionally surrendered, you beat me unconscious and then you kicked the shit out of my groin. You damaged my testicles so severely, they could no longer produce viable sperm. You mashed them with the toe of your boot like a couple of ripe grapes. I woke up to an agony that even to this day is indescribable. After our troops reached POW Camp Twelve, I was sent to a hospital in Tokyo and an army doctor wanted to remove them. I wouldn't let him. They were still partially functional. I could still produce fluid but there were no viable sperm, just cripples who could never swim upstream. You murdered my children before they were ever conceived."

Mishataka had his eyes fixed on the Glock. It was pointed right at his genitals.

"I was married for over forty-six years and my innocent wife never knew. I was ashamed to have an examination, so

98

she accepted it as God's will. My sweet, naive wife didn't know that it was the will of Sergeant Hanaki Mishataka, a fucking Jap war criminal, not her loving God, that she would never be given a child."

Perhaps, Mishataka could now understand the depth of my hate. My words seemed to have reached him. "If I did that, Corporal Foster," he said, "I very much sorry." He bowed deeply.

"When my wife died, my doctor recommended they be removed as they were pre-cancerous. So, I opted for the plastic substitutes. My vanity insisted that I not appear to be less than a whole man. God, what a self-centered decision! I have not been a whole man since August 15, 1945. All because of you."

I felt tears running down my cheeks. Tears of anguish, tears of hate, tears of frustration threaded down my face and dripped into the sand. They made little balls of moisture, unable to sink in.

What good would it do to destroy Mishataka's manhood? He was in his seventies, for God's sake, and certainly had fathered any children he would have. In all probability, nature had already rendered him incapable of fertilization. Outside of rape, what chance did a withered old Japanese ex-soldier have for sexual conquest? Startled, I realized I was also thinking about myself. I turned away from the cage and angrily slung the bamboo cane into the lagoon. Mishataka *still* tortured me.

Mishataka called out, "The past can not be changed. Kill me or let me go. This has to stop sometime."

"True enough," I agreed as I walked away without further comment.

Mishataka watched me until I disappeared into the rain forest at the verge of the sand

❋ ❋ ❋

I was greatly disturbed and a little confused. My latest work with the bamboo cane had not been as satisfying as the first. Maybe it was time for the decision. Now that I had confessed the reason for my fate to the man responsible for it, I did not feel the burden was as heavy as it had been. I knew that it was the first step of closure. For all of his cruelty a half-century back, Mishataka did not seem like a person who still took pleasure from his wartime acts. Instead, he showed a certain kind of dignity that I had not expected. He *had* apologized and his words had a ring of sincerity. They had been spoken with tones of sorrow and regret. What else could he do? Not that I was ready to forgive the Japanese; I just seemed to be losing the desire to torture him. I didn't like that. My anger should be escalating now that I had power over him. My satisfaction should be more satisfying.

As I walked through the rain forest back toward my village, the smells of the vegetation, and low sounds of birds and small ground creatures comforted me. There was vibrant wildlife on Vaka Malua. Innocent life. Why was it that humans were the only animals that practiced unnecessary cruelty? We're supposed to be the highest order of animals. A terrible thought struck me. Was that all we were? Were we animals whose only advantage over the others was a realization that we could doubt our own nature? No, I couldn't let my lapse into uncivilized conduct affect my faith in God. We had to be a step above other creatures. We could sin.

Sin. For the first time in my life I began to think of my actions on a spiritual plane. I am basically a God-fearing man and I know that certain actions, even when they seem to fit certain conditions, are serious offenses against God. Such actions must be grievous in their nature; they must be reflected upon before commission. They must be committed with full consent of one's free will.

Torturing Sergeant Mishataka was certainly a grievous matter and I had given it considerable forethought. Hell, I had planned it in detail. Finally, I had kidnapped him, imprisoned him and beat him with full consent of my being.

That was not like me. How could someone blessed with the lifelong love of a woman like Mary Margaret turn into what I knew I was becoming, an irrational creature of hate, of cruelty, of vengeance? There had to be something else.

"No!" I screamed loudly to the heavens. "Dear God, help me!"

Almost immediately, I realized that all of my rage was not the fault of the Japanese sergeant. He was just the catalyst. Instead, the frustrations of my life were surfacing here on Vaka Malua, brought forth by the contrast between this beautiful, peaceful, unspoiled place and the frantic pace of the business world and advance of society that had consumed my attention for the past half-century. And those frustrations had given the power to my arm as I laid the cane across the back of Mishataka.

My inability to father a child was certainly paramount in my feeling of hate against the old soldier. But my entire life was falling behind me. I had lived through the demise of so many things I had once held dear. My beloved wife was gone, just when we were ready to live out our best years. Apparently, so were the traditional values of my childhood, the integrity and honor between men in the workplace and the sanctity of the male-female relationship. Even my respect for my mother-land that had given me the courage to wade ashore at Okinawa was now departed. All had left me and I had suppressed my despair and disappointment until I had opened Mishataka's green metal box and released my demon.

Now, the revelations of my soul, the release of thoughts and feelings long buried within my subconscious began to drag me back to reality—to *now*.

My cheeks were wet. I thought initially from tears, but an afternoon shower was beginning, the first in four days, and by the time I reached the south beach I had calmed myself. I was also soaked and still partially nude. I had not given a thought to the fact that I had bared my lower body. What did it matter? Unconsciously, I still carried the Glock. I walked into the bar area and poured myself a bourbon and water. There was no need for me to sit with Mishataka around the clock. Let the isolation add to his misery, give him time to reflect, opportunity to regret.

I must decide what to do next. I would get little satisfaction out of further abusing my old enemy. I cursed myself for that.

I had two basic options. Just as Mishataka had claimed, I must either kill him or let him go. I could not accept the first choice even if refusal meant that Mishataka could charge me with kidnapping and assault. Without the *Mary Margaret* at my disposal, I could not release the Japanese and sail away. The eighteen-footer was available and I could travel nearby waters but I would be too visual. The Fijians would have no trouble tracking me down.

My eyes wandering over the lagoon, I mentally talked to my wife. *Mary Margaret, forgive me. I know you would not approve of what I have done. I am so sorry that I never told you why we could not have children. I was ashamed and terribly angry.*

Nothing stirred in my soul. I no longer entertained any feeling that Mary Margaret was present. I could not even pretend the ashes of my wife were still in the lagoon. Realistically, they had dissolved and been swept out to sea by the unending progression of tidal cycles. Minute quantities had been swallowed and digested by the creatures of the lagoon. Even the sand crabs possessed more of Mary Margaret than I did now. Nothing of Mary Margaret remained to offer me solace. She was truly gone. She had been swallowed by the great Pacific, a natural evolution. Did I have enough faith to believe that some day we would be together again? If so, I must not allow myself to miss that ethereal opportunity by my inhumane actions toward a fellow human.

I would have to release Sergeant Mishataka and return him to Viti Levu.

❋ ❋ ❋

My decision made, I had another bourbon and put on a fresh pair of shorts and a tanktop. Once more, I stuck the ziplocked Glock in my waistband and filled the water jug with fresh water into which I dropped several spoonfuls of sugar and a handful of ice cubes.

I walked back across the island to north beach with a renewed purpose. It was time for repentance. I would release Mishataka, give him food and drink and escort him back to the village. There, I would let him shower and I would apply something to the wounds I had inflicted on his back. I was still uncertain as to whether I would call the authorities on Viti

Levu and have them come over or take Mishataka back in the eighteen-footer.

I had a crazy thought that maybe the Japanese would forgive me. It lasted all of a microsecond.

I rounded the last turn before leaving the tree line and stopped in my tracks as I caught my first glimpse of the cage.

It was empty.

No, not again. Oh, shit, oh dear..!

❋　❋　❋

Suddenly, it was very chilly on the north beach of Vaka Malua. I stood by the cage, looking up and down the beach, angry and depressed at the turn of events. Just when I had decided to end this ordeal, Mishataka had turned it into a new contest, maybe one where only death would be the outcome.

How long had the Japanese been free? Which way had he gone? I stooped to examine the cage. I had been certain that no one could get out of it without cutting the lashings and I had made sure that nothing was available to Mishataka. Or had I? Everything was secure until I reached the two hinge lashings. Of necessity, they had been loose and the chain with lock was still in place, but as I pulled on the hinge lines they easily unwound and I could see the severed ends. They were not clean cuts. Could Mishataka have bitten through the heavy nylon cord? Not unless he had steel teeth. There were eight separate wrappings. No way. Then, how did he sever them?

A light as bright as the sun came on in my mind. *Shells.* Somehow, Mishataka had gotten hold of sea shells. That was not far-fetched. You could dig down in the wet sand at any point on the beach and find shells.

I dug one hand into the sand by the cage. At only four inches I found shells, big shells, little shells, tiny shells. And part shells with sharp edges. How stupid could I have been?

Wait! It could be worse. I ran over to the lean-to and searched through my cooking and eating utensils. I had not brought much but I had included a good-sized kitchen knife. It was gone. Mishataka was armed. A water jug was missing. That was about all.

It would do no good to cry out. The Japanese would not answer. It was a new game. I had the advantage of the Glock; Mishataka had the advantage of lying in wait. For the moment, he was also the hunter. But, how strong was he? I had been convinced that I had beat him into an extremely weak condition. Had the Japanese been faking, deliberately appearing to be more wounded than he was? The clever bastard was always thinking, I concluded.

It would be logical, I reasoned, for Mishataka to seek out nourishment. That meant the village. In all probability, he had proceeded in that direction, taking a circuitous route to avoid running into me.

I did not like the idea of crossing the island by the forest trail even though it was the shortest path; there were too many places where an ambush could be set up. The next shortest distance was around the east end of the island, a good hour's walk, maybe sooner if I could jog part time. In the sun, I would have to pace myself. I realized that by the time I reached the village, Mishataka could have foraged for food and either hidden in the complex or vanished back into the rain forest. The situation could result in a waiting game. I did not like that.

Thankfully, I had disconnected all of the communications gear and removed the battery from the eighteen-footer.

It was early evening by the time I came within view of the remains of the boat house. I would wait in the cover of the forest until darkness, then climb into the eighteen-footer, assuming Mishataka had not the same idea, and set up a surveillance of the village. There was a chance that the Japanese had not raided the kitchen and would attempt to do so after dark.

What ill fortune that Mishataka had decided to escape just when I was ready to let him go! I could call out now and broadcast my decision, but chances were that Mishataka would think it was a ruse; I would also give away my presence. No, it would be a cat and mouse game for a while. What would happen eventually, I had no clue. Could the old bastard have enough strength left to overpower me and put *me* in the cage?

Two hours later it was dark enough. Being careful not to present a silhouette, I crossed the sand to the boat and dropped into the cockpit. With my handgun at the ready, I opened the hatch to the cabin and stepped inside. There was a small head forward and I found it empty also. Good. Unless I fell asleep, Mishataka could not board the boat without noisily announcing his presence. I made myself as comfortable as I could and began my watch. The disturbing thoughts I had earlier tried to resurface but I forced myself to put them aside. That was then. This was now. My immediate task was to reverse what had become a very bad situation. Further soul-searching would have to wait.

Eight and a half hours later I was still awake but the night had taken its toll. I had detected no movement within the village area. Stretching and working my limbs to take out some of the stiffness, I realized that Mishataka may have scored the first coup by hiding in the forest and getting a good night's sleep! His body might be weakened but not his mind. I knew that right that minute the old man was plotting his next move.

On the other hand, I was not by nature an extremely patient man. I would wait until noon but no longer. If Mishataka didn't show, I would have to flush him out.

❄ ❄ ❄

The sun was directly overhead. I climbed out of the cabin cruiser and headed for the dining/lounge area. As long as I remained in reasonably open space, Mishataka could not attack me without risking the firepower of the Glock. Still, tired from the lack of sleep and the walk from north beach, I already felt at a disadvantage.

Methodically and with great caution, I entered the kitchen area and checked the pantry. I had just restocked it from the last supply boat and it was obvious that several cans of prepared meat were gone. It looked like some bread had been eaten. Undoubtedly, some fruit had been taken. Dejected, I realized that Mishataka had food, water, a weapon and an element of surprise if I let my guard down. That, I would not do.

Instead, I selected a table in the center of the dining area where I had 360-degree field of vision, fixed myself something to eat, and placed a jug of water and a bottle of bourbon on the table. I put the Glock next to the whiskey.

I sat there most of the rest of the day but about six in the evening, I heard a faint sound. It came again, closer and clearer. It was a voice. It was Mishataka and he was calling from the direction of the rain forest, "Corporal Foster! I am willing to talk!"

I rushed outside. I could see no one nor had I expected to. I responded, "Then, let's talk!" I took a few tentative steps toward east beach.

"You must put down weapon first."

"I will do that but you must also."

"I have no weapon."

I was tempted to charge into the thick undergrowth and spray the area with gunfire but there would be no clear shots and Mishataka could run away. Whether I could chase him and catch up with him was doubtful. A hunting game in the thick rain forest was not to my liking at all. "You sonuvabitch, you have a knife!"

"It is little knife. I put it down when you put down gun."

I did not like the tone of Mishataka's voice. He was up to something. I could *feel* it. "No! We must both be out in the clear. Then, I will lay my weapon down, as will you." I strained to see into the forest but there was no sign of movement.

Mishataka shouted, "If we have no trust, we can not talk."

"You're goddamned right about that!"

I waited for a further response. There was none at first. Undoubtedly, the Japanese was considering his options. His voice returned. "I will meet you on beach by cage. It is wide there and we can see each other well. I will be to west. When I see you on east side and your weapon laid on sand I will expose myself and lay down knife. At that point, we walk and meet and we talk. Agreed, Corporal Foster?"

"Why on the other side of the island?" I asked. "It's open here."

"That is my condition."

Okay, you simple shit. I was back in my hate-Mishataka

mode. I knew what the Japanese wanted, a ritual hand-to-hand battle by the cage. *Bushido* demanded it. It was typical samurai symbolism. It would be risky if that was the case, and I wondered if I could take Mishataka without a weapon. We were both weak. The mere thought of two tired seventy-ish antagonists dukeing it out on the bare sand bordered on the ludicrous. *What the hell!* Initially, I had wanted to beat the shit out of the man with my bare hands. Maybe that was what was going to happen. But first, I would offer to let Mishataka return to Viti Levu and see what the Japanese would offer in return? If that failed, the inevitable could happen. "Agreed, Sergeant Mishataka! By the cage."

❀ ❀ ❀

Once more, I took the east beach route to north beach. I stopped some fifty yards away from the cage and waited. It was later than I thought and the sun was almost to the horizon. I should have thought of that before I agreed to meet the Japanese. A night encounter or even one with reduced light would not be to my advantage. Perhaps, it would be best to convince Mishataka to wait until the morning. Yes, that is what I would do and the old soldier would have to comply. I had the Glock.

An hour passed and I felt the first apprehension at being tricked. The sun had set and the twilight would be gone soon. The sand crabs moved across the beach to the water's edge in the dusky light, beginning their nocturnal foraging.

Damn! I cursed myself for not thinking clearly. The capture and caging of Mishataka had been an ordeal for me also. Had I overdone myself? Were there symptoms of fatigue that I did not yet recognize? I must return to south beach. *Not again,* I despaired, but started the trip one more time around the east side of the island.

※ ※ ※

The first thing I noticed was that the eighteen-footer was no longer moored. Mishataka had taken the boat! How could he? It was too large to paddle. I rushed to the edge of the lagoon and searched out toward the reef. There! In the dusk, almost at the entrance of the lagoon was the eighteen-footer, drifting with the outgoing tide! The strong tide carried the launch briskly toward the open sea.

"Mishataka!" I yelled, throwing myself into the water. After only a few exhausting strokes, I realized there was no way I could catch the cabin cruiser. It was entering the narrow channel and the Venturi effect of the funnel of water was drawing it seaward with ever increasing speed. I could not see if anyone was on the boat but it was obvious. Mishataka had lured me away long enough to steal the boat and somehow had gotten it far enough out into the lagoon where the ebb tide took over.

I treaded water, feeling the fool that I certainly was.

Someone would run across the drifting cruiser, most probably during the next day, and recover Mishataka. He would tell his story and the authorities from Viti Levu would come to Vaka Malua and arrest me. All was lost and it was lost through stupidity. That was what hurt.

I returned to the beach and watched until I could no longer see the eighteen-footer. My only solace was the bourbon, which didn't erase my feeling of incompetence but did flavor it with the bitter humor of the situation.

It was well into early morning when I finally succumbed to sleep and it was a deep sleep with only a short REM period when I dreamed of Mary Margaret.

We were at sea on our sloop and it was night. We were seated in the cockpit and Mary Margaret was resting her head on my shoulder. "I want a child," she said.

I couldn't respond.

"I want a child," she repeated. "We are not a family until we have a child."

"Oh, Mary Margaret, I wish so much that I could give you one. I cannot."

She wrestled herself away from me and stood. "You do not love me!" she screamed into the empty ocean.

"I do, I do!" Looking beyond her I saw a figure standing on the foredeck. It was Sergeant Mishataka and his taunting laughter drowned out my words. "No!" I yelled and rushed forward. Just before I reached him, he held up a clenched hand; it was holding my testicles-filled scrotum. Enraged, I dived toward him. He merely stepped aside and I plunged over the bow.

Underwater, I could look up and see the keel of the *Mary Margaret* passing over me. I slammed my hands over my ears to drown out the echoing laughter of my demon.

Then, there was a black nothingness.

The sun was already climbing well above the eastern horizon when I awoke. My eyes were stuck shut from a mixture of sand dust and tears that had oozed out during the night. It took me a while, perhaps several minutes before I could force them open. I could see the lagoon beyond the entrance to my *bure* and hear the soft whish of low surf wetting the sand.

Sergeant Hanaki Mishataka of the Army of Imperial Japan, sat in a wicker chair, facing me. He held the Glock loosely in his right hand.

"*Ohiyo goe zaimas, Foster-san,*" the Japanese said. Despite the cordial greeting, he was not smiling.

CHAPTER 7

SEPPUKU

At first, I thought I still might be dreaming. Then, I prayed that I was. Finally, I realized that I was not. I sat up and twisted to place my feet on the floor.

Mishataka had on a clean loincloth but nothing else.

"Why didn't you kill me while I was asleep?" I asked.

"Why should I kill you? You did not kill me."

"I thought I might, at first."

"What happen?" he asked.

"It would serve no purpose. I am not a murderer."

Mishataka grunted. "Hah, you not very good prison guard, either. If I had cane, I would have beat you until you pleaded for mercy. I would never have walked away leaving you able to even stand."

"You did that, fifty-three years ago."

"That is what I would like to talk about."

I tilted my head toward the Glock. "You have the floor."

"Despite my cruelty to you, I am not bad person. I serve country, I raise children. I came to know America and Americans. I had remorse but history is history. We lost tragic war. We were disgraced as only Japanese can be. You cannot understand that."

"I can come close. During the years I have known Japan and the Japanese."

"But even your surrender to become prisoner of war did

not disgrace you?"

"I didn't surrender. I was captured while unconscious."

Mishataka nodded in understanding. "In my culture, even that would have been disgrace. Tell me, once you came to know us, what did you think?"

"I found your people during the occupation years to be honorable, family-oriented and extremely motivated."

"Like Americans."

"True enough, I suppose."

"And now?" Mishataka asked.

"You're on a mission. It's costing you your souls but in return you will become the leading Pacific Rim power. It's a tough trade to evaluate from an American viewpoint."

"You no longer have respect for us?"

"That's not correct. It's just a different kind of respect, combined with sort of a wariness."

"What about you and me?"

"What do you mean?" I asked.

"What has brought us to this point in our lives? It is incredible."

"I don't know. What difference does it make?"

Mishataka stood, looked at me for a long minute before stepping over and offering me the handgun. "I think our mutual destiny started in 1945 and inevitably led us to this island where we now find ourselves. It is fate, maybe kismet or as your Doris Day once sang, 'Que sera, sera'. There is purpose to it."

Mishataka was familiar with Doris Day? I laid the Glock on the bed. "I don't think I know what that is."

"There has been mutual bitterness. We both look back on

those days with regret and sorrow, for vastly different reasons. It has been hard for us to let go. It was most important event in our lives. Still, when all things are considered, it may have been the best years of our time. We each lived up to our own code of honor and integrity."

I could agree with that.

Looking away, Mishataka mused, "I read somewhere that every hundred years, world is populated with completely new people except few who live beyond century mark. Very few. Interesting concept, *hai*? A whole new world full of people. All others gone."

"What's the point?"

"We mean nothing anymore, Corporal Foster, except maybe to each other. Perhaps, we're just two more sand crabs on a faraway beach. Can you see that? Each of us is a means to our private resolution of failures in life. I fail to serve emperor. You fail to serve wife by not giving her children."

"I failed because of you."

"That is true. It doubles my shame."

I had to share some of that blame. I had been less than honest with Mary Margaret. She would have understood.

Mishataka went on, speaking slowly and with consideration of each word, "I think maybe we have been destined to be here on this day, in this place, since we left mothers' wombs. Every man has destiny; yours and mine have wound through the years, each ignorant of the other, and just seem to have collided here in most unlikely place."

"For what purpose?" I asked. "You think there is a preordained reason for this?"

"Yes. You can now take comfort from your revenge. I have opportunity to redeem myself as warrior."

"I don't understand," I said.

"You are not Shinto."

"No."

"You are not samurai."

"No."

"When samurai meet honorable opponent, there is great respect and overpowering urge to kill opponent for in victory there is pride of service to master."

"The Emperor," I offered.

"In 1945, yes. All Japanese soldier think they samurai. Almost all fight and die according to code of *bushido*. I could not."

"Why is that?"

"I had no enemy to fight. I was garrison soldier, prison guard. I could beat and torture out of contempt but my order was not to kill. I took out frustration on you and others."

"I can understand that but I don't accept it as an excuse for what you did to me."

Mishataka appeared not to hear my remark. Mentally, he was somewhere else. "I could not die in battle. My soul could not join the other honorable warriors at the Yasakuni Shrine on Kudan Hill in Tokyo. That is where our heroes rest."

"I know that."

"Then, you know I must kill you or be killed in battle of honor. I have not sought this. You brought it to me. After all these years, I have final opportunity to fight, perhaps die for my emperor."

116

"Your emperor died years ago. Akihito does not demand the same service. As you have pointed out, we are history. Well, I'm not going to fight you. If you wish, I will call the authorities on Viti Levu and they can come and get you. You can prefer charges. My score is settled."

"No! We resolve our differences here, now. It is opportunity neither of us anticipated. We are among last warriors of Great War. Out here, on this island, our generation no longer exists as such. There is only you and me."

For the first time, I realized that the chance encounter between Mishataka and me had been a golden opportunity for the Japanese as well as for me. I could not even begin to imagine the odds of such a thing happening. It was surreal.

Mishataka leaned across the chair. At that moment, I noticed that a bottle of sake and two shot glasses were on the side table beside it. The rice wine was probably Mishataka's private stock. It was the same brand he had served in his apartment and I had noticed it in our bar.

Mishataka poured two shots and handed one to me. "We toast to one of us who dies this day on the sand and becomes food for the creatures who feast on such things. *Kanpai!*"

I refused to raise my glass.

Mishataka's eyes flashed angrily as he hurled his empty glass across the *bure*. "I will wait for you. Shoot me if you wish. But when you leave this *bure*, be prepared to defend yourself." With his last word, Mishataka whirled and purposefully stomped down the steps to the beach. He continued on for another twenty feet. Then he turned to face me, spread his legs and folded his arms across his chest.

I stood in the entranceway. "I said I will not fight you."

"You are not coward."

"No, I am not. But I am also not a fool. Our score is settled. Look, Sergeant, let us live out our days as worthy adversaries who have seen the error of our ways."

"Do not deny me this. I beg." He spat the word like a curse.

I looked at the pitiful figure standing on the white sand, a withered banty rooster with delusions that he was still a soldier of the empire, an old samurai desperately longing for some dignity. How our relationship had changed, going from retribution by me to a plea for salvation from Mishataka. I walked down the steps, crossed over to stand less than an arms length from the Japanese and swung a right cross with such ferocity that I was as startled as he at the force of the impact. The old soldier dropped like he had been sandbagged.

"Now," I said, wincing from the pain in my knuckles, "I'm going over to the bar, sit down on my seventy-one year old ass and pour myself a bourbon and water. You can join me if you wish. I'm going to drink to the demise of the World War Two generation, of which you and I are pretty goddamned sorry representatives." I really meant my words. We were relics of the past, as germane to the world as the sand crabs that surveyed the fallen Mishataka with their long-stemmed eyes.

❀ ❀ ❀

Mishataka sat up on the sand but did not move while I finished a pair of two-finger bourbons. Then, he rose, disappeared into my *bure* for a few moments and emerged carrying a sheet and the kitchen knife he had stolen from the lean-to. He could have killed me without the Glock while I slept.

Carefully spreading out the sheet, Mishataka sat in the exact middle and bowed his head in prayer before straightening up and putting the point of the blade of the knife against his lower left abdomen.

Seppuku! "No!" I shouted and ran out toward Mishataka.

"One step farther, I die," the Japanese announced.

"All right. I'll fight you."

Mishataka worked his sore jaw and a trace of a grin flickered across his face, but only for a moment. Then he spoke.

"Our great General Hideki Tojo wrote book before war, Sanjin Kun; translation: The Ethics of Battle. In book, he say 'Do not stay alive in dishonor.' He would not be proud of this soldier".

I held up my hands. "You are no longer a soldier. Don't do this. Think of your grandchildren."

"You must help me. The ritual requires second person, a fellow warrior."

Now, I was trapped in a Japanese opera. I tried to stare into Mishataka's eyes and read his soul. Surprisingly, I felt I could. I found determination there, in the set of his shoulder and the firmness of his jaw. The old man was going to die, here on Vaka Malua, in the presence of an enemy he had once despised but now asked for assistance in an honorable death. The eyes were pleading. *Do this for me. Help send me to the Yasakuni Shrine.*

The confusing thing was that I wanted to help him. I

understood the old man's wish. My abuse of him had taken him back in time just as it had me. We were both on the same side of the door. "What do I do?" I asked weakly.

"Kneel close to me. Grip knife and help me pull across stomach. Then, in true tradition, you must cut off head but that is not possible with this little knife. So, you must place bullet in back of my neck, just below skull."

"I don't know if I can do this, Sergeant Mishataka."

"You will do fine, Corporal Foster. Now, when I say, help me pull blade."

My hands were sweaty and trembling much more than his but I managed to kneel before him and grip his fingers. The touch of our hands completed an unlikely bond that had been born of hate so many years back. For a brief moment, we were warrior brothers. There was a short pause before Mishataka spoke, "You honor me, Foster-san." Then, he uttered a crisp, "*Hai!*"

I felt him plunge the knife into his body and I followed his pulling motion. The knife sliced open his abdomen with amazing ease. Mishataka's entrails spilled out onto the sand amid an outpouring of thick red blood. The instant stench caused my nostrils to recoil.

Mishataka was bent double. He gasped in pain. "Now, the bullet." He hissed the words through teeth clenched in agony.

Oh, shit! The Glock was in the *bure*! I hurried and retrieved it. Without further delay, I placed it as the Japanese had instructed, jerked back the slide to load and arm, and pulled the trigger. There was no clip! Mishataka must have unloaded it and I had been in too big a hurry to check.

120

With his last effort, Mishataka raised his head slightly. "Foster-san," he whispered with great pain and just a trace of a smile, "I think maybe you fuck up two-car funeral...*kanpai*." He pitched forward and was still.

CHAPTER 8

THE INVESTIGATION

I gagged but did not vomit. It took a few minutes, but somehow, I mustered sufficient composure to lay Mishataka on his back and loosely stuff his severed intestines back into the abdominal cavity. Before pulling the sheet over the body, I washed in the lagoon. Then, I returned to my *bure* and removed one of the white pillowcases from the bed. In the supply room, I found a can of red paint. The label appropriately described the color as Sunset Red and the small can had been used to paint certain items in the village that required CAUTION indicators, like the rectangular floor area around the wall-mounted fire extinguishers, for example.

I laid the pillowcase across one of the dining room tables and carefully outlined a red circle in the middle. It wasn't a perfect circle but I was able to adjust it as I filled it in with a heavy coat of the red paint. Holding the case at both ends to avoid smudging it, I returned to the sand and placed it lengthwise across Mishataka's wrapped body. It seemed fitting. Standing erect, I rendered my best memory of a Marine Corps salute. I still did not fully appreciate the Japanese tradition of honor and death in battle but it had been a burning concept in the mind of Sergeant Hanaki Mishataka.

I would have to report the suicide to the authorities on Viti Levu. But first, I felt a need to just sit on the sand beside Mishataka and let my mind unwind. It was full of contradictions and half-thoughts. When I had first arrived at Vaka Malua, I had sensed it was the place of my ultimate destiny. Perhaps, it was. Perhaps, it was only a waypoint.

I tried to keep the last days in perspective but they had been so completely unpredictable that I wondered how they could ever have happened. Only a few days back, I had sailed into the lagoon of my paradise with no concerns except the grief over the loss of my wife. Vaka Malua was supposed to ease that. Instead, other memories had surfaced and complicated my life. I was falling into a deep pit of depression.

I started to cry. Although there were several reasons why I should do such a thing, I couldn't attribute the tears to any single cause. I was so lonely without Mary Margaret. In a strange, haunting way, I was homesick. I was profoundly ashamed of my kidnapping and torture of the Japanese. I was abysmally disappointed that my visit to Vaka Malua had changed from hope and a promise of comfort to unreasonable rage and inexcusable conduct. I was now a man I would never have thought I could be.

I sat there for a long time, until the sun began to settle on the western horizon. The brilliant blue of the Pacific sky seemed to tire and reach for a long night's sleep. At first, its fade was almost imperceptible as traces of orange and yellow appeared and began to bleed across the heavens. I began to pray.

"Oh, my God, I am heartily sorry for having offended you...."

The fuzzy bottoms of the clouds on the western horizon began to brighten while the billowing tops fought to retain the brilliance of the last low rays of the sun. The towering cumuli captured the last sunlight, becoming iridescent in a display of color of such intensity that I realized I was praying in a vast outdoor cathedral.

"...and I detest all my sins, because I dread the loss of heaven and the pains of hell...."

The reds appeared and gently spread across the western sky, absorbing the yellows and oranges and mixing them into a horizontal blend of color that was neither red nor orange nor yellow yet was all three, so perfectly combined that they became a single swath of indescribable beauty. The emerging deep red reached out and enfolded me.

"...but most of all because they offend You, my God, who are all good and deserving of all my love...."

The whitecaps in the ocean beyond the reef picked up the red tint of the sunset as did the white sand of south beach.

The sky was now primal red, a reflection of the time of the origin of Man as well as a reminder of his adventurous side, his aggressive warlike nature and his willingness to die for what he believed in.

"...I firmly resolve, with the help of Your grace, to confess my sins, to do penance, and to amend my life. Amen."

I had not recited the words for over fifty years but each one had come to me as clearly as did the realization that, in being exposed to the character of Hanaki Mishataka, I could forgive him. It might take a while longer to forget. The first part of that process would be to contact the authorities on Viti Levu.

The easiest method would be by cellular phone and I dialed the number for the police headquarters in Suva. The answer was immediate.

"Suva Station. How may I help you?"

"This is Donald Foster on Vaka Malua. I wish to report a suicide."

"Yes, Mister Foster. This is Sergeant Bakito. You have a *suicide* on your island?"

I remembered the jovial police officer. We had met several times since our original contact in 1994 when I negotiated the purchase of my island.

"Yes, Sergeant, a Japanese national by the name of Hanaki Mishataka. He is better known on Viti Levu as Mirata Nakai."

"Nakai? We have been looking for him. He disappeared from work on the eighteenth. Mister Dobson at the Hilton reported him missing. When did this happen?'

"Just a short while ago."

"You found the body?"

"I witnessed the suicide."

"I see. You are sure he is dead?"

"Perfectly sure."

From the background noise I could tell that Bakito had already fed the information into the necessary network consoles and the police were preparing to leave for my island.

Bakito's voice returned. "Are there other witnesses, Mister Foster?"

"No, there is no one else on the island. I have no transportation."

"I understand. Where is the body?"

"It is lying on the beach in front of my village. I have covered it."

"That is good, sir. Do not touch anything else. Are you all right?"

"Yes, I'm fine." *Well, not really.*

"An investigative team is on the way, as well as a representative of the coroner's office. They should arrive by helicopter in about twenty minutes. I'm sorry, Mister Foster, to hear about this tragedy."

"*Vinaka*," I murmured, laying down the handset.

There was nothing to do now but wait, and consider what would happen next. There would be extensive questioning; I knew that, and it would serve no purpose to speak other than the truth. I did not want to say anything that would incriminate me and I did not want to feel that I was directly responsible for Mishataka's death. But I was certainly instrumental. For God's sake, I had even helped him pull the knife across his belly. And I had certainly precipitated the whole affair by kidnapping Mishataka and torturing him.

Amazingly enough, I was not too concerned about what the future held for me. I had resolved the most tragic issue of my life by confronting and repaying the Japanese for the pain and suffering he had inflicted upon me. We were even. As I had that thought, I knew it was childish of me. Getting even was such an immature way to resolve conflict. Thank God, in the process I had learned that. Now I faced the consequences. I realized that the overriding consideration was that I no longer felt any animosity toward Mishataka. If anything, I pitied him while at the same time admired him for such strict adherence to his traditional principles.

Actually, we were quite a bit alike, both of the same generation and both suffering some disillusionment with developments in our respective countries. I suspected that he was as unhappy with the changes in his culture as I was with those in mine. If one really thought about it, I think the conclusion would be that we both migrated to this remote corner of the South Pacific for similar reasons.

Fate is such a mystery, all of the myriad of events that happen to one in a lifetime leading to unexpected paths, completely new challenges, and in the case of Mishataka and myself, such impossible coincidences. Any slight deviation in either of our lives would have disrupted the destinies that had brought us together and we would never have met again. But that hadn't happened. For over a half-century, one thing had lead to another, and that to another, and so on, as unstoppable as the wind. All things for the both of us had led us to Vaka Malua.

Two helicopters arrived twenty minutes later, the first a police vehicle, the second the hotel chopper sent by Charlie Dobson and piloted by the cocky Aussie who had flown me before. He climbed out of the helicopter but remained standing next to it.

As the main rotor wound down, four figures emerged from the police helicopter, one in plain clothes, two uniformed officers and one in a white coat carrying a black rubber body bag. I waited by Mishataka's body. There was still a trace of twilight and I had lit the beachfront torches and turned on the outside village lights.

The plain-clothed figure introduced himself, "Mister Foster, Detective Tom Mara." He was a tall handsome black man with piercing deep brown eyes and a large nose that housed full nostrils. He had thick lips and a perfectly round cut of black kinky hair confirmed that he was a pure Fijian. He carried an air of no-nonsense authority with him as he walked over and uncovered the body. "Hara-kiri?" he asked, using the more familiar western term.

"Yes," I answered.

He glanced at the painted pillowcase. "He made the flag?"

"No, I did."

"I see. Is there identification?"

"There is a metal box of personal papers in the main hut with an ID card as to his identity as Mishataka. Also, some papers confirming he was using the name Nakai. I'm sure that there are several people on Viti Levu who knew him as such."

As he motioned for one of the officers to get the box, Mara asked, "Which one was he to you?"

"I knew him under both names."

Detective Mara slipped on rubber gloves and picked up the kitchen knife. I had left it beside the body. "Is this the weapon?"

I didn't particularly like the phrase "the weapon." I had not thought of it as such. "Yes."

Mara dropped it into a large ziplock bag held out by one of the officers. "What a way to do it," Mara commented. "Mister Foster, I must ask you to come back to Viti Levu with us. We will need a formal statement."

"I understand."

"I can leave one of my men here to insure the security while you are gone."

"I would appreciate that," I responded.

"Of course."

The man in the white coat and one of the police officers had placed Mishataka in the body bag and zipped it closed. Now, they were loading it onto the police helicopter. Detective

Mara called the Aussie pilot over and addressed us both, "Take Mister Foster back to the Fiji Hilton. We will complete our preliminary investigation this evening and if you will, Mister Foster, please come to the station tomorrow morning at eight o'clock. You may prepare your written statement before you come if you wish. I would recommend that, since the events of this evening will be fresh in your memory."

"I'm not under arrest?"

"No, of course not. You are the only witness we have to Mister Mishataka's suicide, that is all. I would think we could have this matter cleared up by tomorrow evening."

I tried to read Mara's face. What was he *really* thinking? How much investigative experience did he actually have? He had the demeanor of a professional. I doubted that he would accept Mishataka's suicide at face value but he did not seem to be considering any other possibility at the moment. He was not even going over the premises. I did note that the police officer returning to Suva was taking my makeshift Japanese flag. I was thankful I had returned the Glock to my bure. It could have raised questions.

As we walked over to board our respective helicopters I spoke to the officer remaining behind, "There's plenty food and drinks in the kitchen. Please help yourself. I normally don't burn the electric lights all night but feel free to leave them on as a security measure. No one comes here; the passage through the reef is a little tricky when it's dark."

"*Vinaka*," the officer replied and started over to the lounge area.

We took off in trail behind the police aircraft.

"You've 'ad a bloody bad night, myte," the pilot ventured.

130

"'e laid 'imself wyde open, 'e did. Just sit back and try t' relax. I'll giv' ya a good smooth flight back t' Suva. Mister Dobson is waitin' fer ya."

It was the longest fifteen minutes I had ever been in the air. I was being taken out of my environment in the dark of the night. I tried to busy myself by searching for the lights of ships and boats below but there were only a few. The chopper was noisy and shook. Strange, I hadn't noticed that before.

The silver lights of the city appeared, dotted in the central area by the various colors of neon, and the pilot descended to place his charge in the middle of the hotel pad with just a bare bump. Charlie Dobson took me by the arm as I climbed out of the chopper. "It's a terrible thing, Mister Foster," he said. "Are you all right?"

"Yes, just a bit rattled, maybe. It was not a pretty sight. I...I helped him, Charlie."

"Oh, great God! Don't tell that to the police."

"I don't intend to."

"We've been worried about Nakai, ever since he disappeared," offered Dobson. "I tried to check with you but no one has been able to raise Vaka Malua on anything."

"I had everything shut off for a while. Maintenance reasons."

We passed through the lobby and Dobson stayed with me until I reached my suite.

"I'll leave you here, unless you want to talk," he said.

"No, not tonight. I have to prepare my written statement."

"That's good. I'll send you up some dinner."

"That's not necessary. I'll order from room service later. Thanks, Charlie."

"You're more than welcome, sir. Call me for anything."

"Charlie?"

"Yes, sir?"

"Nakai's real name is Hanaki Mishataka. I'll explain it to you later."

Dobson was understandably surprised and confused but he accepted my offer to inform him later of what had happened.

Inside, I changed into a pair of pajamas. I always kept a small wardrobe in the suite. As always, the wet bar featured my favorite bourbon and after pouring a drink I sat down at the desk and prepared to write my statement. What was I going to say?

❋ ❋ ❋

I arrived at police headquarters promptly at eight and was ushered into an interrogation room. Detective Mara was waiting and rose to greet me with the more formal, "*Ni sa Bula.* Can I get you some coffee?"

"*Bula.* No, I had some at the hotel." I placed my statement in front of him.

"Thank you." He gave it a cursory glance and set it aside. "Our discussion will be taped. Do you have any objections to that?"

"No, of course not."

"Mister Foster, the coroner's preliminary findings confirm that Mister Mishataka apparently died of a self-inflicted wound to the abdomen. There are other findings that puzzle us. For example, the body has severe lash or whip marks on the back. They appear to be quite recent. Would you care to comment on that?"

Before I could answer, he held up a hand in warning.

"I should mention that you may have legal counsel present if you wish. We, of course, have the British legal system, quite similar in principle to what you enjoy in the United States but there are differences in procedures that you may not be aware of. We have no Miranda requirement, for example. We have no prohibitions against self-incrimination such as your Fifth Amendment to your Constitution. Also, at this point, this remains a routine police investigation. It does not require you to be placed under oath."

Was Mara offering me a chance to lie? Or was it a form of entrapment? I had stayed awake most of the night trying to decide how I would respond to this morning's inquiry. I had known the coroner would find the marks on Mishataka's back and most probably discover that he had been malnourished and possibly dehydrated. At first, I thought I might be able to come up with some kind of cover story but soon realized that what had happened would be obvious. Besides, I was unaccustomed to lying. I would tell the truth but it must be the whole story. My written statement had only covered the act of suicide and my observation of it. I had not mentioned my participation.

"I am responsible for those injuries," I admitted.

"Are you sure you do not desire legal representation?"

"No, provided you hear me out. I would like to start at the beginning."

"Please do."

It took a while, thirty minutes, while I revealed to Detective Mara the story of my 1945 mistreatment at the hands of Mishataka in POW Camp Twelve, the resultant loss of my ability to father children, my incomplete marriage to a woman whom I dearly loved, and the long years of anger and regret. I told him of how I had come into contact with Mishataka, Nakai at the time, and what an improbable event it had been. I told him of my intent to make Mishataka suffer as I had and how in the process we had reconciled ourselves to the tragedies we had both undergone. Mishataka's answer had been ritual suicide. Mine had been forgiveness. Mara sat fascinated with the story, not saying a word. When I finished, he turned off the tape machine.

"The cage. You kept him in the cage?"

"For a while. At his pleasure, I lived in a similar one for seventy-three days in 1945."

Mara rose and walked over to a window. "My father was a coastal watcher in World War Two. He worked with an Australian and they reported Japanese military movements in various parts of the South Pacific. He used to tell me stories. Over 5,000 Fijians fought with the allies in the battle for the Solomon Islands. The survivors still tell tales hard to believe." He returned to his chair. "You know that you have committed a very serious assault upon the person of Hanaki Mishataka."

"Yes, I do."

Mara turned on the tape again. "How did Mister Mishataka come to be on your island?"

"I met him at the Hilton and asked him over." I knew that was a bit of a stretch but I was not yet under oath.

"Did he go willingly? His apartment seemed to have been vacated in a hurry. There was food on the stove and partially eaten meals remained on the table."

"I persuaded him by telling him I wanted to show him what I had accomplished since he had left my service."

"At that point, did he know that you knew he was Hanaki Mishataka?"

"No," I answered. No need to admit that I had been addressing the Japanese as Mishataka at that point.

"Once you arrived on Vaka Malua, what came next?"

"I put him in the cage and showed him the papers and ID card."

"Did he recognize you?"

"I don't believe he had any idea who I was until I identified myself to him."

Detective Mara walked over to a bottled water stand and drew a paper cup full. "Want some?" he asked.

"No, thank you."

"How long did you keep him in the cage?"

"Four or five days. I'm at a bit of a loss as to the time. He escaped, actually, as I told you a few minutes back."

"Oh, yes. He had an opportunity to kill you, did he not?"

"Definitely."

"You stated a few minutes ago that you beat him with a piece of bamboo, you deprived him of food and water. Is that correct?"

"Yes."

"Did he make any attempt to fight back?"

"Only after he had escaped and confronted me at my *bure*."

Mara leaned on the table. "I must urge you at this point to seek legal representation. I do not wish to question you further without that. It is your right."

"My attorney practices in Honolulu. I would prefer him."

"Then, I suggest you call him immediately. If he is not licensed to practice in the Republic of Fiji, I'm sure the court will appoint a local solicitor and they can work together."

"You intend to charge me?"

"My investigation is not complete. I propose to suspend it until you have legal representation."

"That is very considerate."

Once more, Mara turned off the tape. "Mister Foster, you are well known in these islands to be a friend of Fiji. You have contributed significant financial support to several of our most needy charities. From what you have just told me, you intend to live among us on a permanent basis."

"I hope to."

"My job at this point is difficult. I can understand how you hated Mishataka and I can see why you did what you apparently have done. I am in sympathy with that but my obligation to enforce the laws of the Republic of Fiji must override any personal feelings I have. I have tried to look at this from the standpoint of a delayed action of self-defense but I could never sell that to our chief prosecutor."

I needed to stand and stretch. "I fully understand. My purpose in being so candid with you is to insure that this whole miserable episode in my life is looked at from all viewpoints."

"I am certain, Mister Foster, that you will be charged, at the very least, with assault and battery. There are possible manslaughter implications. Possibly kidnapping."

"The man was a war criminal."

"That is not a matter for us to consider."

"Then, I must call my attorney."

"You must also remain on Viti Levu until I can meet with you both," Mara stated. "You have your passport with you?"

"It is on Vaka Malua, in my *bure*. What will happen to Mishataka's body?"

"It will be turned over to the Japanese Embassy here."

"If there are any expenses, I should like to cover them."

"That won't be necessary."

Back at the hotel, I immediately called Honolulu. I knew that I should not have volunteered so much information about my actions. That was not smart and Jacob Mikimura would dress me down for that. He started as soon as I gave him the bare bones account of what had happened and what I had told Detective Mara.

"Holy Christ, Donald, you should not have admitted anything. We're starting off at the bottom of a deep pit."

"How soon can you be here?"

"Next flight out, probably tomorrow. But we've a serious problem. I'm primarily a corporate lawyer. You know that."

"Charter a plane if you have to," I directed. "I want you down here. If we need someone else, we can handle that later."

Mikimura had the best legal mind I had ever encountered and he had some criminal law experience as a younger man. I also knew that he had traveled all over the Pacific in his legal capacity. I could picture him, sitting there in his office, holding the phone and shaking his head in exasperation at my dumb responses to the interrogation.

However, he was still the professional. "I'll check on the caliber of Fiji legal talent in Suva and we can select someone after I arrive. I have connections who will help us. Have you notified our embassy?"

"No."

"Do that right away. Meanwhile, don't talk to anybody else. I'm surprised. You're smarter than that."

I deserved the rebuke. I was just not myself.

✳ ✳ ✳

Jacob Mikimura arrived shortly after noon the next day, his flight landing at the Nadi airport. I met him with one of the hotel cars.

"Hello, Donald," were his first words. His next went right to the point. "I've engaged the best criminal law solicitor in Fiji, Radhi Nehru, an Indian of some reputation."

I asked, "Should we see him before we see Detective Mara?"

"I don't think we have to as long as our discussions remain on an investigative level. If it gets serious, then we pull in our Indian big gun. I'd like to stop by the hotel to freshen up and we can see Mara as soon as he's available."

I phoned Mara and made the appointment while Mikimura shaved and put on a fresh shirt. We arrived at the detective's office in mid-afternoon and I made the introduction.

Mara responded, "Pleasure to meet you, counselor. I assume Mister Foster has informed you of the basic details."

"Yes, I think so."

We all took our seats around a small interrogation table. The room was well lit, not at all threatening and there was ample natural light coming in through two large windows that overlooked the government buildings of Suva.

Mara continued, "What we have here is an apparent suicide. The complications arise from the personal relationship of your client with the deceased prior to the death. There is evidence and Mister Foster has confirmed that he assaulted the deceased prior to the suicide. I do have a few more questions before I present my report to the prosecutor's office and I will be taping this interview if you have no objections."

Mikimura acquiesced, "No objection. I do reserve the right to advise my client as I feel necessary."

"No problem, there. Mister Foster, we found your fingerprints on the handle of the knife used."

It was not asked as a question but Mara obviously was anticipating a reply. So, I made one. "It was one of my kitchen knives. I have handled it on numerous occasions."

"Some of the prints were on top of the blood stains, sir."

"I also handled it after Mishataka died. I had laid it beside the wrapped body as you will recall."

Mara nodded.

"Mister Foster," Mara continued, "I asked the officer we left on your island to bring me your passport. I assume that was all right."

"Yes, of course." I loved the Fijians. Mara had every right to confiscate my passport, yet here he was, soliciting my permission as if he had just borrowed a cup of sugar.

"In the process of retrieving it, he came upon a nine-millimeter Glock semi-automatic handgun. It has been recently fired. Did you threaten the deceased with it?"

Mikimura interrupted, "You don't have to answer that, Donald."

I didn't mind as long as I was not under oath. "I have fired it in the past few weeks. I'm afraid that I don't clean it as often as I should." I wasn't lying.

"Mister Foster, did you kill Hanaki Mishataka or assist in his suicide?"

That was the question I knew would be coming. "I did not kill him."

"Did you assist in his suicide?"

Mikimura was shaking his head. He did not feel I should answer that.

I did not want to answer the question directly; I wanted Mara to worry about what I would say if we went to trial. "I would think that would be a more appropriate question if I am charged with a crime related to the suicide." A "no" answer would be of no value to the case and I was certain that he wanted a solid finding before he referred it to the chief prosecutor.

Mara did not seem to be disturbed by my legal sidestep. Nor did Mikimura.

Mara addressed his next question to Mikimura. "How well versed are you in our system of law?"

"It's based on the English system. On Mister Foster's behalf I have employed the services of a local solicitor in the event charges are made. He would be the primary counsel."

"May I ask who that is?"

"Radhi Nehru."

Mara smiled. "You have good judgment. Mister Nehru is much respected."

Mikimura was more blunt. "Are we going to need him?"

"Yes," Mara answered. It was the first time that he had indicated he intended to prefer charges. "Mister Foster, at this time, I must place you under arrest for assault and battery upon the person of one Hanaki Mishataka and for the crime of second degree manslaughter in connection with his death."

I did not expect the manslaughter charge.

"I will recommend that you be released on your own recognizance. You are well known here in Fiji and I believe you deserve that trust."

"What happens next?" I asked.

"I will make my report with recommendations that I have just stated. You will be required to appear at a preliminary hearing where you can enter your plea."

Mikimura asked, "When can we expect that hearing?"

"It will be a decision of the court. It depends upon the magistrate assigned to the case. His clerk will advise you."

"We request permission to await notification on Vaka Malua," I said.

"That is possible. The prosecutor's office will make that decision and notify you. Until then, you must remain in Suva, at the Hilton, I assume?"

Mikimura answered, "Yes, that's fine. Thank you. Is that all for today?"

Mara nodded. "Yes, I will make note of your cooperative manner."

❋ ❋ ❋

Back at the Fiji Hilton, I suggested that Mikimura share my suite. There was ample room and extra sleeping facilities. Charlie Dobson invited us to have dinner. I knew he was as curious as a cat in a room full of rubber mice about the details of my situation.

At dinner, he announced, "We have your cabin cruiser in the marina. It was turned over to us after I identified it. The marina operator has installed a fresh battery. It's none the worse for wear after a solo day at sea."

"Thanks, Charlie. We may be going over to Vaka Malua for a couple days. If so, we'll take it back."

"The chopper's available."

"No, you've done enough for me."

We had been back in my suite for almost an hour when the phone rang. Mikimura answered it. It was a clerk at the office of the chief prosecutor. They talked a few minutes before Mikimura hung up the phone and briefed me on the call.

"You're cleared to wait on Vaka Malua for the arraignment, day after tomorrow. I have to go over and sign some papers in your behalf. I'll also stop by and talk to Nehru so he'll be up to speed."

"He won't be in his office this late," I commented. It was almost nine o'clock.

"I have his home phone and address. I'll catch him."

I should have known.

❋ ❋ ❋

Jacob Mikimura was suitably impressed as soon as he saw Vaka Malua. "My God," he exclaimed, "this *is* Paradise."

"A term I use quite often."

We left the eighteen-footer in the storm damaged boat house slip and I waited in the lounge while Mikimura stowed his few things in one of the *bures*. We had left Viti Levu in the late morning and it was lunchtime. I fixed us a couple of canned meat sandwiches and joined Mikimura with a beer as we ate.

"You know, Donald," Mikimura began, "I've never seen such a relaxed investigation of what could be a major crime. Detective Mara is one laid-back officer of the law. And the prosecutor's office, hell's bells, it was more like you were being charged with a parking violation. I signed a few papers. Didn't have to show any ID."

"You should get to know the Fijians. They abhor violent crime and drug violations. They can be extremely harsh in prosecution and sentencing, believe me. But they are the most friendly, hospitable and relaxed of all the Pacific natives. Don't let that fool you. Our next appearance will be all business I assure you. And I'm worried."

"Forget the manslaughter charge. Nehru agrees with me that they don't have a case. No witnesses. No evidence except the knife and there's a perfectly good explanation for your prints. By itself, it's not even good circumstantial evidence."

"And the assault charges?"

"You confessed." I knew Mikimura wanted to say more on that subject but he contained himself. "We go for mitigating circumstances."

"There may be another favorable factor."

"What is that?"

"The Fijians are not particularly fond of the Japanese."

Mikimura shrugged. "That shouldn't be a factor in the letter of the law. I'd like to meet with Nehru tomorrow."

"We can go over in the morning."

"No. Just me. We need to bond," Mikimura said, grinning.

"You talked to him last night."

"Yes. He's okay, precise, methodical, crafty. The prosecution will have one worthy adversary. We'll make a good team, Donald. He knows the intricacies of the Fijian legal system and I know you."

"What do you think are my chances?"

Mikimura ignored the question, "Beer in the reefer?"

"Yes. Help yourself. It's in the small room behind the kitchen." Why hadn't he answered my question? He was being

143

cheerful enough but that could be for my benefit. I repeated the question as soon as he returned, "What do you think of my chances?"

"Worst case? Manslaughter? As I said, forget it. Assault? First time offender, your age, both pluses. Your confession will probably kill us. There's damning evidence: the wounds on Mishataka's back, the cage. According to the Fijian code for such an offense, max penalty could be a stiff fine and five years imprisonment. I would hope for no more than two, maybe suspended. I'm sorry to be so blunt but you asked and I think you should be aware of what you're involved in."

"Does Nehru agree?"

"That's what I need to talk to him about."

"How about a plea bargain?"

"Don't know the Fijian attitude toward that. I'll discuss it with Nehru."

"Well, come on," I suggested, "let's take a walk around my island. It'll relax us."

"Going to show me the cage?"

"Highlight of the trip...."

Mikimura spent the next day in Suva, working with Nehru to set up our defense strategy. I had difficulty in understanding how such a thing could be done without me being present but I didn't want to question them at this point. I could use the time alone on my island.

My life had changed; I should have known that it would the moment I had realized that Nakai was Hanaki Mishataka.

144

No longer could I look forward to immediate retirement on the island. Instead, I was most probably looking at several years in prison. I didn't know anything about Fijian prisons although I suspected they were more primitive than ours. I doubted I would have the privileges and safeguards of U.S. facilities. Yet, I knew the Fijians to be good people, a great number of them under Christian influence.

I spent a lot of the time overlooking the lagoon, as was my habit when I had some serious thinking to do. Perhaps, I should contact Niko and Sarah and have them return and care for the island while I was away. If not, Sammy Kamehame was probably still available. I could leave either of them a list of things to be accomplished and by the time I was released, Vaka Malua could truly be in its primal state except for my living quarters.

No matter how hard I tried, I could work up no enthusiasm for alternate plans. The changes to my village at Vaka Malua, while a major goal, were now in the background. A few days back, I would not have imagined them to be a secondary consideration.

I wondered if Mary Margaret was aware of what was going on; what would she think? I doubted that she would have approved of my abuse of Mishataka; she was far too gentle a person for that. But maybe she could have understood my satisfaction, and my current dilemma did nothing to diminish that. The demon in my mind that had been Mishataka was gone. If someone earlier had asked me if I would trade several years of my life, even if spent imprisoned, for a chance to confront Mishataka I would have replied with a resounding, "Yes." Why not accept that same decision now?

❄ ❄ ❄

I made a mental note to express my appreciation to Charlie Dobson for all that he was doing for me. He was my only real Fijian friend.

Mikimura returned on the Hilton's helicopter just before sunset. He briefed me on his talks with Nehru.

"Arraignment is still scheduled for tomorrow at ten. We've drawn a Magistrate named Henry Takanua. He has a reputation of being fair, but a stickler for procedures and formalities. Nehru has argued a number of cases before him and is not concerned. But he does have some reservations about the charges. The prosecution is going to include kidnapping and manslaughter."

"I thought those were tossed out."

"So did I. And I still don't see any purpose in including them. They just don't have a case there, Donald. Maybe, it's to influence the court and jury even if the charges are dropped."

"They must have something," I cautioned.

"God only knows what it is, then." The attorney shrugged. "Incidentally. I keep hearing the term 'white Fijian' tossed around. Is that a derogatory term here?"

"Not exactly. A white Fijian is just that, a Fijian citizen of Caucasian birth. Normally, an immigrant and there aren't a lot of them. I suspect the Fijians regard them as something less than a native citizen, possibly because of the way the Indians multiplied after they arrived and took over the country. The Fijians finally had enough of that and it ended with the coup. There aren't enough white Fijians to create that type of problem. When I become a citizen, I'll be a white Fijian. I'll be very proud of that for it is a select group."

"How about a felony conviction?"

I hadn't even considered the impact of that upon my plans. "I don't know but it could disqualify me. God, I'd be crushed."

"You could still stay on Vaka Malua as an American."

"It wouldn't be the same."

Mikimura placed a hand on my shoulder. "Then, I guess Nehru and I are going to have to get you a good solid acquittal."

I wished he had sounded more convincing.

CHAPTER 9

THE TRIAL

Magistrate Takanua's courtroom was spotless. The dark-lacquered nineteenth-century period bench, tables, witness box, jury section and seated spectator area were reminiscent of traditional British courtrooms. I almost expected to see Charles Laughton in a long white wig seated in judgment while John Mills prepared to argue my case. Everything was polished to a high sheen and the members of the court were impeccably clothed in black robes and powdered wigs.

My arraignment took only twenty-five minutes. I found Judge Takanua just as Mikimura had described him. Takanua read the charges and addressed me in a booming baritone voice that made me look twice to make sure that it was not the dignified American actor, James Earl Jones, who was speaking. There was a remarkable resemblance except Takanua's nose and lips were broader.

"Mister Foster," he asked, "do you understand the nature of the charges being preferred against you?" He was an impressive man on the bench, large, erect, proper with dark eyes that burned into mine as if they were projecting laser beams. Like Detective Mara, he was a proud native Fijian and his courtroom reflected his demeanor.

"I do, your honor," I replied.

"How do you plead?"

"Not guilty, sir."

Takanua added, "I understand you wish to waive jury trial?"

"That is correct, sir."

Takanua thumbed through an appointment calendar and selected a date and time.

"Mister Nehru, is the twenty-fifth agreeable to the defense?"

We could go to trial in three days? That was unheard of in US courts and it was completely contrary to the Fijian way of doing things. Tomorrow was always a better day to do things even if it never came.

Nehru answered in his high pitched and precisely correct English, "That is agreeable."

"Then, we shall make it so, shall we not? Ten a.m. on Friday, September twenty-fifth. Next case, please."

I had to ask Nehru, "Three days does not seem to be a lot of time, does it?"

"You have told us everything?"

"Yes, of course."

"Then, I am ready to go to trial."

I looked at Mikimura.

My Honolulu counsel added, "Despite the serious charges, the defense is straight forward. We're ready." He explained further, "We can counter the kidnapping and manslaughter charges; they're just smoke. On the assault charges, as you and I previously agreed upon, you will have to take the stand."

I realized that. There were no witnesses to my World War II treatment at the hands of Sergeant Mishataka. There was the medical report filed by the medics who examined me immediately after my liberation from POW Camp Twelve. Amazingly, Mikimura had been able to obtain a fax copy of the 53-year-old document from the Navy Department immediately after I had first talked with him. It was evidence of mistreatment but not of the identity of the perpetrator. Even if it were, would it have been strong enough to establish a mitigating circumstance?

I had earlier reasoned that my defense was to be based on emotional appeal. But did Nehru know Takanua well enough to risk such a ploy? The big Fijian did not appear to me to be someone who would be unduly influenced by emotion.

I did not feel that race would be a factor. The Fijians were not racists, but they did harbor resentment against the Indians. And would Takanua be looking at me as a prospective white Fijian? Citizens of such heritage and background were tolerated but certainly not sought. Especially ones with a violent nature and it must appear to the court that I could be one of such a bent.

We continued our conversation outside the courtroom. Nehru also reassured me. "In Fiji, a trial is not a contest of solicitors to see who is the most effective. It is not a legal show of cunning and innuendo, as it tends to be in the United States. The caliber of the solicitor is certainly a factor but the goal is truth and justice. You must also remember that the Fijians remain a tribal society and tribal concepts are very much present in the philosophy of our legal system. Justice is normally swift, in contrast to the Fijian way of life. But it could be worse. In the old days, for a violation of tribal laws you could be killed and eaten."

"What the hell does that mean?" I asked, perplexed.

Nehru laughed. "In the United States, you have a saying: go with the flow. That is what we will do. The court will grant us additional time if we express a need for it."

Nehru led us to a small consultation room down the hall

from the courtroom. There was a water stand in one corner and I drew a paper cup full, downed it with one long swallow and drew another.

"Mister Foster," Nehru began after we were seated around a small conference table. "We really have two avenues of defense. The first is to play upon the inherent justice of the Fijian system, to argue that your mistreatment of Mishataka was a delayed but justifiable reaction to your treatment at his hands in the World War Two prison camp. I would present that argument as a mitigating circumstance.

"We feel confident that such an approach could call for a suspended sentence and possibly could result in a verdict of not guilty."

"Possibly?" I questioned.

Neither of the two gave me a verbal answer. Mikimura did shrug and raise his arms as if to say, "It's possible."

"What's the other tack?" I questioned.

Nehru answered, "Change your plea to not guilty due to temporary insanity, brought about by the shock of meeting Mishitaka after years of shame and suffering. You momentarily snapped."

I would not admit it aloud but in my mind that is exactly what happened. I did lose all sense of reason and responsibility. I wanted Mishitaka's ass and I went after him in spite of my deep down residual feeling that it was not right.

"What kind of verdict could we expect?" I asked,

Nehru clasped his hands in front of his chin. "In that case, we must take a chance on the inner feelings of Magistrate Takanua inasmuch as we have waved a jury trial. I would expect that there would be a reasonable chance of a 'not guilty by reason of insanity' verdict. There would be provisions, of course."

152

"Such as treatment," I surmised.

"Yes."

I turned to Mikimura. "What do you think, Jacob?"

"If we were in the States and had a hand-picked jury trial, I would still go for mitigating circumstances. We would insure the jury was packed with World War Two vets or spouses. We can't rely on that here, so you might want to reconsider and go for temporary insanity. Odds are you would escape any prison time."

"Do we have an expert witness who could testify as to my mental state?"

Nehru's soft smile preceded his comment, "We have a medical expert who, upon examining you, I am sure would support our argument."

I mentally weighed the two courses of action while Nehru and Mikimura waited patiently.

"Why didn't you advise me to plea temporary insanity to begin with?" I asked Nehru.

"We discussed it briefly. You will recall we briefed you on it as a possible plea, but with little emphasis since we agreed that there is a chance we can come up with a 'not guilty' verdict to a straight 'not guilty' plea."

"Based on just my testimony? We have no other witnesses or evidence."

Mikimura answered, "This whole case is based on your testimony. The prosecution has no witnesses, either."

"They have my confession or what amounts to my confession."

"True, and that's the point. We want to turn that admission around to support the mitigating circumstance argument. What man would not have done what you did under identical circumstances?"

"We turn around the prosecution's main argument to our favor," Nehru emphasized.

"So, we stay with my plea?"

Nehru replied, "Yes. It is our intention to have the court absolve you completely. Otherwise, your desire to become a citizen of the Republic of Fiji will be in jeopardy. An admitted case of temporary insanity would not look good on your citizenship application form."

"Conviction of a felony doesn't really enhance it," I countered.

"We agreed before," Mikimura reminded me. "No second thoughts, Donald. We can do this."

❋ ❋ ❋

The next day we spent in a rehearsal for the trial. Nehru and Mikimura made me go over and over my story of abuse at the hands of Mishataka. Each alternated as the prosecutor and by the time of my last free evening we all felt that we had covered every eventuality. Nehru was ready with counter-arguments for every conceivable prosecution argument. As we rehearsed, I came to see that the trial would be a very basic one with no complicated conspiracies or complex testimony. It would be my testimony against my confession and the prosecution's material evidence.

❋ ❋ ❋

Magistrate Takanua swept into the courtroom like a large black cloud and banged his gavel as he sat.

"This court is in session," he said, "in consideration of the case of the Municipality of Suva against Donald Foster concerning the charges of kidnapping, assault and battery, and second degree manslaughter. Is the prosecution ready?"

"We are, your honor."

"And the defense?"

"We are, your honor."

"We have two defense motions before the court; to dismiss the charges of kidnapping and manslaughter due to lack of evidence. The motions are approved."

The prosecutor jumped to his feet. "The prosecution wishes to contest your decision, your honor."

Takanua looked very annoyed. "Do you have any solid physical evidence that Mister Foster at any time forced Mister Mishataka to accompany him to Vaka Malua other than what you have proposed to place into evidence by your pretrial brief?"

"No, your honor."

"Do you have any physical evidence or testimony other than the fingerprints on the knife, which can be easily explained away?"

"No, your honor, but we feel...."

Takanua was obviously in a non-feeling mode. "Motions are granted. Is the prosecution prepared to present its opening argument on the assault charges?"

I was stunned. Sure, Nehru and Mikimura had assured me that those two charges bordered on the frivolous and could not be supported. I was not that confident but Magistrate Takanua was obviously of the same mind as my legal counsels. I felt like a football coach who had just seen his team score a touchdown before the fans had seated themselves after the opening kickoff.

"The prosecution is ready to proceed, your honor."

"And the defense?"

Nehru answered, "We are ready, your honor."

Takanua settled himself in his high backed leather chair. "I will hear the prosecution's opening statement."

The prosecutor stood and fixed his eyes on Takanua. "If the court pleases, the prosecution will show that Donald Foster did entice Mirata Nakai, more properly known as Hanaki Mishataka, from his residence here in Suva on the evening of September 14, 1998, and did take him to the island of Vaka Malua. There, Mister Foster did willfully assault and torture Mister Mishataka by confinement in a bamboo cage, physical beatings and the denial of food, water and sanitary conveniences. Mister Foster then assisted Mister Mishataka in the ritual Japanese suicide known as seppuku. Thank you, your honor."

"That was quick," I commented to myself.

"Mister Nehru?"

Nehru stood and adjusted his lightweight coat so that it hung precisely right. "Your honor, the defense will show that the charges of kidnapping and manslaughter are without any substantiating evidence or testimony and I respectfully remind the court those charges have been dismissed. As to the charge of assault, Mister Foster was merely responding to the brutal treatment he had received from Mister Mishataka while a prisoner of war, such treatment in violation of the Geneva Conventions. We will present mitigating circumstances that show, without a doubt, that Mister Foster was fully justified in his actions with respect to the treatment of Mister Mishataka. We will also demonstrate that...."

Takanua was visibly annoyed as his clerk leaned over and

whispered in his ear. Nevertheless, he immediately stood and announced, "I regret that an interruption is necessary. This court is in recess for ten minutes. Mister Nehru, you will be allowed to repeat your opening statement as you desire." The magistrate banged his gavel sharply as he left for his chambers.

Eleven minutes later, he returned.

The clerk announced, "This court is back in session, Honorable Henry Takanua presiding."

Magistrate Takanua leaned forward from his chair, eyes narrowed and eyebrows arched. "Is the defense ready to resume its opening argument?"

"Yes, your honor," Nehru answered.

"Well, the court is not!"

Nehru and Mikimura sat with faces certainly as confused as mine —and the prosecution's, for that matter.

"Will counsels approach?" Takanua had phrased a question but his tone defined an order. Nehru joined the prosecutor in front of the judge. Takanua spoke with them quietly for a moment but his face was animated and not as pleasant as I had observed in the past. He gave them each a folded paper that appeared to be a summons or testament or maybe a deposition, but such a procedure was not the court's role. As the two per-plexed men returned to their respective places, Takanua announced, "In my court, I expect all of the parties involved to have prepared themselves to the fullest. That is necessary for the court's proper consideration of evidence and testimony. It has come to my attention and I am not pleased that both of you have overlooked a determinable piece of evidence in this case. You have five minutes to study the passages on that document that are outlined in yellow."

Nehru and Mikimura were already devouring the words of the indicated paragraphs like a couple of jackals on a fresh kill.

"My God, I never would have thought of this," Mikimura muttered.

"Neither did anyone else," Nehru observed. "This settles the case."

He looked at me, about to burst with the revelation of what was in the paper. I could see it was a copy of my deed to Vaka Malua but I had no idea of what it could contain that would have any bearing on my trial. Before Nehru could speak to me, Takanua roared, "This case is dismissed. I will see both counsels in my chambers, *now*."

A thunderbolt in the form of one pissed-off judiciary had entered the courtroom and thrown out all the charges against me in a matter of minutes. I could not even react.

Takanua repeated in a loud voice, "Now!" as he disappeared into his chambers.

"I better go," Nehru stated with nervous haste, "Jacob, you explain to Mister Foster."

Mikimura was beside himself with elation. "You live a charmed life, Donald. This is one for the books."

"What the hell is it?" I pleaded.

Mikimura spoke very deliberately, "This court has no jurisdiction over you in this matter. Who was the lawyer that handled your purchase of Vaka Malua?"

I had to think for a moment. "It was a young Indian, just out of law school, ah, name of, ah, Sikha. Yes. I don't recall his first name. He had specialized in property law. A very personable young man."

"And either incredibly brilliant or as dumb as a stump,"

Mikimura commented.

"I don't understand."

"He not only provided you with a bill of sale that includes Vaka Malua but also states that the island is deeded to you....here, let me read, '...deeded in perpetuity, such deed to include absolute ownership of all land and improvements plus *exemption of the Republic of Fiji in the determination of the rights and privileges applicable to the land, including legal arguments, unless said arguments involve the rights and privileges of citizens of the Republic of Fiji.*'"

"It sounds awkward."

"It is, but it is very definite in its meaning. This deed, in effect, removes the sovereignty of Fiji over Vaka Malua. And it is signed by a qualified official of the Republic who must have had his head so far up his ass he could examine his own stomach contents. You have your own little country, Donald, my friend."

"Fiji has no jurisdiction over my island?"

"No sovereignty, no jurisdiction unless it concerns a Fijian citizen. Mishataka was a foreign national."

"I can't believe it."

"Well, Takanua just confirmed it."

I felt so light-headed I was afraid my body would float up from my chair. "How did the judge know of this? Where did he get copies of my deed?"

Mikimura threw up his hands. "I haven't the slightest idea but I bet Nehru is getting the word right this minute in no uncertain terms."

As if on cue, Nehru returned, "Mister Foster, Magistrate Takanua wishes to see you. I would advise you not to delay."

Still in the dark, I knocked and walked into Takanua's

chambers. I feared his anger would be directed toward me. Quite the contrary, he greeted me warmly and handed me a tall frosted glass of fresh lemonade. "Fine drink," he commented, "especially if made with Florida lemons. Ours just aren't the same."

I was ready for it.

"Mister Foster, you are the beneficiary of a monumental mistake in the drafting of a legal document." The smile was still on his face so I began to relax as he continued, "I just had a call from the office of General Rabuka. You have his great respect and admiration and he speaks highly of you."

"I am a fan of the General. He is a national hero."

"Yes, and when he speaks, we listen, even those of us in the judiciary. We have maintained our tribal loyalties to our chiefs and he is our greatest chief. His messenger was waiting in my chambers and at the general's request, he brought your deed to Vaka Malua to my attention."

So, that was how it had gotten into the magistrate's hands.

"He also suggested that you be spared any further inconvenience and embarrassment. I regret you had to undergo such an ordeal and you have this court's apology."

"That is not necessary, your honor. I am very grateful of course to both the general and you."

"It has been our duties. Candidly, I am amused at such improbable circumstances and I should tell you that I suspect we will take legal steps to revise your deed. I feel you will be understanding."

"As a prospective citizen, I have no problem with that," I answered. It was right that Vaka Malua remain within the domain of the Republic of Fiji even though I would continue to be the legal owner.

"I preached a bit to your counsel and the prosecutor. Have to maintain my image, you know. Also, young solicitor Sikha will have to appear before a special committee of the bar. Who knows how much of Fiji he has given away!" Takanua stiffened his back and let his grin expand until I felt it would wrap around his great head. "Perhaps, you could join me at dinner some time," he invited. We could make it a real *meke*, a traditional feast, in your honor as a new citizen. A real celebration."

"That's a promise, your honor."

Takanua gracefully escorted me to the door.

"*Vinaka*," I said. I left the magistrate shaking his great head like a black lion of state. Nehru and Mikimura were still waiting in the courtroom.

"I am truly sorry," Nehru stated.

"I never thought of checking the deed. How did Takanua get it?" Mikimura asked.

"General Rabuka gave it to him. I suspect he had a hand in the drafting of the document. It was overly generous. Best $200,000 I ever spent," I said, recalling my financial support of the general's coup. "Whether the sovereignty clause was intended or not, we'll never know, but it'll be revised. The magistrate indicated that."

"Well, you were king for a day, or an emperor or a president. Whatever," Mikimura joked.

"Let's go get a drink," I suggested.

Nehru heartily agreed, "That would be nice. A cup of hot tea, perhaps with wild herbs and some biscuits. If you will permit me, I know just the shop."

Tea with wild herbs and biscuits? I wondered if the proper and polite Indian ever loosened up. Even here in Fiji, he was still closer to Britain.

CHAPTER 10

RESOLUTION

It has been almost two years since my encounter with Sergeant Mishataka and the Fiji court system. I have left my island only four times in that interim.

I am now a white Fijian and my compact village has been reduced to only the main hut and one *bure*. From two tall bamboo flagpoles anchored in front of the main hut, I fly both the flags of my native country, the United States of America, and my adopted land, the Republic of Fiji. They are constant reminders of my heritage and my future, limited though the latter phase of my life may be. Over on north beach, at the foot of the stand of bamboo that is nestled within the dormant volcanic rim, I have placed my cage and from it I fly a small flag of Japan. I visit the site on occasion and renew my apologies to Sergeant Mishataka for my mistreatment of him. He is no longer my demon, of course. His ashes were returned to Japan right after the trial and I trust his spirit is present at the Yasakuni Shrine in Tokyo. If not, to hell with him.

Charlie Dobson has stopped by on two occasions, the last just a few weeks back. Leoa was with him; she is working at the hotel now. They brought me a bottle of Early Times and I didn't have the nerve to tell them I have two cases in the storeroom. Charlie also sends me little gifts of food from time to time on the weekly supply boat which brings me my major replenishment items. A couple months back, he took me with him for a day's sail aboard his ketch and the familiar feel of the open ocean was exhilarating. I still maintain my suite at the Fiji Hilton and I have forbidden him to send me any newspapers or magazines.

Shortly after my revised deed was actuated, General Rabuka flew over on a military helicopter. He remains the Prime Minister. He presented the deed to me with a flourish and an impish grin to share his recognition that I had temporarily beaten the system. He also brought a mini-feast of Fijian food and six precious Fijian children who entertained us with native dances and songs while we ate. It was a true *meke* celebration. The sight of a menacing six-year old warrior holding high an authentic and quite heavy war club while dancing bare-footed toward me amid his swishing grass skirt was an image I shall always remember with relish.

Even Sammy Kamehame, hosting a bevy of young female Japanese tourists, whizzed over one Sunday late last year in a rented powerboat. He showed them around the island but I was careful to caution him about the cage on north beach. The young ladies swam in the lagoon and I fed them lunch. In typical style they feigned coyness and delicately covered their mouths when they giggled, which they did frequently at Sammy's antics.

I do feel a bit greedy, having the mangrove crabs all to myself. I eat one on special occasions such as my birthday, my wedding anniversary and the Fourth of July. Otherwise, my fare is simple, lots of fruit, an egg from time to time and most often fresh fish from the lagoon. I miss Manalo's ocean-fresh, red-meated *ahi* and the subtle use of natural herbs that was a hallmark of Sarah's cooking when we were at sea.

Niko and Sarah sailed the *Pa'aloha* into the lagoon eight weeks back and introduced me to their daughter, a precocious fourteen-month old petite Polynesian princess who has the innocent soul of an angel, the twinkling laughter of the tooth fairy and the mischievous dark eyes of the Hawaiian Goddess, Pele. She quickly decided that I was her personal manservant. I took her by the hand and we toddled down to the water where I showed her the fishes and we waded together. It was a glorious experience and my reward was a series of gripping hugs and a very moist kiss on my cheek. They left the next day, and my little princess called out "Bye, bye, Gampa," on cue from the departing Zodiak. I cried with both happiness and sorrow as I watched the lapping lagoon wash away her tiny footprints. My precious Polynesian family promised to come back, but life is full of twists and turns.

I often think of Mishataka's remark that the world has a completely new population every hundred years and that has prompted me to take stock of what my generation is leaving behind. Almost all of us who still survive are in the seventy- to eighty-year age bracket so our century-successors are about to take over. We have been the sons and daughters of the Great Depression and the first truly global war. We set foot on the Moon and weathered the stressful thirty-year Cold War. We lived through the shame of the Vietnam conflict and watched our government intrude more and more into our daily lives.

Yet, we have seen our nation become the most powerful and influential in the world. In the process, we have lived through a major cultural change in the behavior and lifestyle of our beloved country. We are on the verge of becoming a participant in a new world order that will cost us part of our precious national sovereignty. Do we really want that?

History will probably put it all in proper perspective after a century or two. But I will always think of our generation as a people who were of admirable moral character, who met the challenges of our day with determination and turned back threats to our nation with a rolled-up-sleeve type of patriotism. I shall always love the United States of America but I shall shed tears whenever I think of what she has become.

I know that may seem a strange comment coming from an American who lives in Fiji but the truth is that I could not find this type of serene existence anywhere in my native land. Things are just too out of control there. Even my former resident-state, Hawaii, which still maintains a traditional Polynesian presence, has succumbed to all of the mainland ills. They are evident in varying degrees, depending upon which island you visit.

I prefer my tiny Fijian island. Besides, dying here on Vaka Malua will be merely a short trip from one Paradise to another.

Ordinarily, I would have kept my thoughts on such weighty subjects to myself but last week I had a visitor, a young woman journalist from *Time Magazine*. Somehow, the editorial staff there thought my self-imposed isolation on Vaka Malua might make an interesting human-interest story.

She had a catchy name, Venture Harris, and she hired a boat to bring her over to my island. An attractive brunette with sparkling brown eyes, in her early thirties I would guess, she wore khaki shorts and a T-shirt; both were offensive to the modest Fijians. She strode confidently across the sand and held out her hand. I took it, perplexed that in such a warm and pleasant place, it was the hand of a corpse. It was cold, with no grip whatsoever.

After introductions, we sat in the open dining area. We sipped diet soft drinks and she interviewed me. We covered the incident with Mishataka in some detail and she listened intently, occasionally nodding her head and uttering a nondescript "Uh-huh" as she held her palm-sized tape recorder in her lap. She asked no questions but indicated that the tragic encounter would be her lead-in.

"World War II foes turn a chance encounter into a resolution of old differences," was the way she phrased it. Then, she went right to the main interest of the interview, "Why have you decided to give up life in your native country?" she asked.

"I haven't given that up," I answered. I had not expected such a inconsiderate opening inquiry. "As I have aged, I have found myself to be out of the current mainstream of America. My reliance on family values has been shattered. Indeed, my concept of the family no longer exists in the majority of US homes. Progress has outstripped my ability to adjust and I believe that destiny did indeed bring me to Vaka Malua and my encounter with Hanaki Mishataka. He took me back to my formative days and I began to realize that I was not seeking out the solitude of a Pacific island for the purpose of living a life I would have preferred to experience with Mary Margaret. No, indeed!

I believe my subconscious brought me here out of frustration and an inability to cope. I suppose I got tired of fighting the good fight. For the first time in my life I felt powerless to achieve anything of substance. Like Mishataka, I have become too traditional and perhaps, I must admit, too chauvinistic."

"Could you be more specific?"

I was not sure I wanted to go into detail. Too often in the past, I had been misunderstood. But she seemed sincere enough at the moment and here was an opportunity to express myself in a national magazine. So, I responded.

"There are so many things. As a businessman, I have been unable to adjust to the fact that the gigantic influx of women into the workplace and their on-going battle to achieve equality — whatever that is, in their minds —has produced a social structure where there is constant political strife based on gender."

"You don't believe women have the right to pursue the same goals as men?" Venture asked.

"I don't look at it as a matter of right. Certainly, they have that right. But for many women, it's a choice and not all of the choices that we make in life are good. In my day, women were almost sacred. They were the sweethearts, sisters, wives and mothers of us all and we males, despite our crude manner and dirty work clothes, looked up to them."

Venture gave me a very condescending smile. "That's a bit idealistic, don't you think?"

"No. Women were on pedestals, the givers of life and the perennial nurturers of it. They were without a doubt superior to us in moral values, civilized conduct and compassion for their fellow man. Now, they are merely equal."

"And you feel we've changed?"

I preferred to keep the interview in the third person. Venture should have, also. Otherwise, her objectivity could suffer. I started to address that but decided to just go on with my answer. I knew I was walking a very thin line between honest concern and insensitivity.

"For the last quarter-century, women have been struggling

up the corporate ladders, becoming pioneers in medicine and science and developing skills formally thought to be exclusively masculine. Today, they catch crooks and fight fires. I applaud them for expanding their horizons, I really do, but they've left a big gap in family life. Who is going to fill that? I miss the pedestal. And you know, I don't think the ladies fell off. I believe they jumped. And a great number jumped before they looked at the consequences."

I could see that I was not impressing Venture.

"Woman are entitled to equal opportunity," she stated firmly, her eyes beginning to narrow.

"Of course they are. But it is not just a matter of equal opportunity. There are serious social consequences to any large adjustment to what have been traditional lifestyles."

"Such as?" She raised an eyebrow.

"In the area that concerns me, increased competition for available jobs. Deterioration of the family structure. Latchkey kids. Aren't we getting off the subject?" I asked. "I thought this interview was about my life on Vaka Malua. I'm not sure my social commentary is of interest to your readers." I had certain reservations about how I would be quoted but I did not intend to hold back my beliefs.

Venture sensed blood. "I think it is about to become the central theme of my story. It's what has driven you into this isolation, isn't it?"

"Perhaps, in part."

"You're an ex-combat marine. How do you feel about women in the military?

"That was a long time ago."

"You must have an opinion," she insisted.

"I do. I have difficulty with the abandonment of the concept that the protection of the family and the nation is no longer the prime responsibility of the male. Physiologically, historically, traditionally and evolutionarily, that male obligation has always been present. I've never considered that concept to be a claim of gender superiority, just a fact brought about by males. Males have bigger necks, stronger backs, less common sense and a certain instinctive proclivity to tests of strength, the ultimate being combat, which is to say, warfare. I'm not sure that you can equate female-acquired skills such as operating highly technical land and air military vehicles and manning ships of the line with the male's primal drive to push the edge of the combat envelop. Obviously, I have not been a popular dinner guest back on Oahu."

"Why is that?"

"I tend to express my concern about statistics that show fourteen percent of our fighting personnel are female. I don't see female participation in the rougher male contact sports such as football, ice hockey and rugby. When did we suddenly begin to define hand-to-hand combat as less demanding than those brutal encounters? I know that I would have been much less confident wading ashore on Okinawa if better than every tenth marine had been female. We no longer have a lean, mean, fighting machine. Too many of our soldiers, sailors, marines and airmen are wholly or partially incapacitated by pregnancy, menstruation, PMS and family leave."

"Spare me, *pulleese!*"

"Miss Harris, I don't intend that to be a sarcastic statement, just a dose of realism and a slice of life. The military did not have to contend with it during my tenure. Anything that detracts from a combat unit's readiness and ability to fight must be carefully evaluated."

"You are blunt, aren't you, Mister Foster? However, you seem to be ignoring the achievements of female combatants in the Gulf War."

"Don't misunderstand me. Women have served admirably in the military, either in an auxiliary or direct service, since our country was founded. The Continental Army had several female combatants in 1776; were you aware of that? I have absolutely no objection to women in the military, *per se*. In fact, I'm not sure that in the volunteer military, we can accomplish our mission without them. My objection is the current drive for unrestricted combat assignments. As for the Gulf War, there were heroic performances by a number of females, God bless 'em. But, it also caused a lot of them to reevaluate their career choices. In all fairness, that observation probably applies to a number of the male military, as well. But, that wasn't much of a war compared to World War Two or Korea or certainly, Vietnam. I don't belittle the Gulf conflict. Brave men and women died. But I do not consider it a comprehensive test of female military combatants."

Venture was having trouble remaining cordial. "Did *you* serve in that conflict?"

She knew I had not. "No. I was an overage established business man way before that time."

"I'm sure you were disappointed."

I looked closely at her mouth to see if I could detect fangs.

"Tell me, did your business experience have any bearing on your decision to retire here?"

I was glad to get away from the military discussion.

"Good question. I haven't really thought about that much but I guess that over the years, as a businessman who had to wrestle with the technological and social changes taking place in the workspace, I've lost my desire to compete. I do not see our computer-oriented business society as the most effective or most efficient. We can certainly keep better records and accurate inventory but we generate more paperwork, not less, and the keyboard has replaced face to face negotiation and human exchange.

"I'd like to add another thought. We've lost personal consideration of one another in a society where sexual permissiveness has reached an all-time high and yet we are completely Victorian when it comes to matters of sexual harassment, especially in the work area. What is the logic of an attitude that sees nothing wrong with someone screwing whomsoever they please —excuse my French —on practically any occasion but rushes to court the poor soul who happens to tender an innocent wink or several unsolicited invitations for dinner? What happened to healthy flirting and courtship?"

"You seem to always get back to the female-male thing, Mister Foster."

I had to admit she was getting to me. "It seems that I do. But there are other equally disturbing considerations."

"Social?"

"Yes. It has dawned on me that there is one other reason I have come to Vaka Malua. It is because I am helpless to restore the level of education and health that our children used to enjoy. I have money and I have spread a good portion of it around to causes and agencies that are formed for the express purpose of helping children learn and remain healthy.

"Yet, they remain the dumbest, most neglected young Americans in our history. Oh, they have modern skills. While they may have trouble expressing themselves, reading, writing and working with mathematics, they are well versed in how to slip on a condom or use other means to insure safe sex. Even then, we have children bearing children on a nation-wide scale. Have you ever *really* thought of that, Miss Harris?"

"I still hear the anti-feminist speaking."

"That's your interpretation, not mine. Let me tell you something else. In too many cases, our children are taught revisionist history that is diagnostically flawed instead of historically accurate. Instead of applauding our brightest and most promising students, we lower our educational standards so that all of our pupils can experience a sense of accomplishment. Believe me, my *failures* in life have made me appreciate accomplishment all the more. If Mary Margaret and I had produced children and grandchildren, how would we have coped?"

"I suspect you would have had a great deal of difficulty." Venture switched off her tape machine and stuck it in her shoulder bag, much as a victorious Amazon warrior would holster her sword.

"I assume the interview is over," I remarked.

"Yes, Mister Foster, it is. I don't see a story here, just a bitter old man, quite probably a racist murderer with lots of money, who resents the fact that women are no longer barefoot and pregnant."

I could only take offense at such a ridiculous statement. "You have no right to say that, Miss Harris. I've been candid and honest. You haven't been listening. I'm disappointed with you and the magazine that employs you."

Venture Harris looked at me as if I were a bug she would like to step on. "Enjoy the rest of your miserable life here. I don't believe America will miss you," she concluded, walking away.

I am seldom rude. I did stand as she left but I did not escort her to her boat. She never looked back at me or at Vaka Malua.

I knew there would be no article about me in *Time Magazine* but I suspected there would be an editorial comment. The young woman and I had touched on some sensitive areas and political correctness would undoubtedly inspire her. How closed was her mind! She was the loss to society, not me.

❉　❉　❉

With all of my frustration and disappointment, and I've come to realize that my Mishataka nightmare was really only a part of that, I am still very proud to have been an American, to have been a US Marine. I still consider myself both. I feel privileged to have had the opportunity to shed blood for the country of my birth. In that respect, I am but one of millions of men and women who lived through my time with a profound sense of honor, dignity and accomplishment.

But I am also proud to be Fijian, to live among a branch of the Pacific people who have not lost all of their childlike qualities. The great Pacific Triangle encompasses one of the last truly native populations of this Earth, people who before the jet age, remained untarnished by technology and pollution and are now with renewed purpose striving to preserve their heritage.

They are fighting a losing battle, of course, but as long as they persevere, I shall be on Vaka Malua, doing my bit and cheering for their success.

I am at peace here. My generation had its chance and we truly tried. I wish I could know what has gone wrong. In any event, it is now up to Venture and her contemporaries. I wish them well.

I read a lot, write some, paint a little—seascapes as you might expect. Some of them are passable for an old man of limited talent. I talk to God on a spontaneous basis, this outdoor cathedral reminding me of His constant and concerned presence. Obviously, I do a lot of thinking. The sea winds and the clear, unpolluted atmosphere that washes over Vaka Malua, along with my lovely loneliness, stimulates thought, even meditation. Sometimes, introspection.

Sometimes, I fear that I have copped out and my life now is very selfish. I've given up the fight.

I hope not. I am caring for a piece of Mother Earth, protecting it, nurturing it, enjoying its beauty. I still have considerable financial resources and steady income from investments. At the end of every year I allocate a proper proportion of my wealth to those less fortunate than I. I am doing good and the only question is: am I doing all the good that I can?

My bottom line is that I have adjusted to things I cannot change and wish the rest of my life to be one of contemplation and contribution.

My reward is Vaka Malua. I am continually serenaded by the optimistic sounds of its birds and small animals and even insects. Every morning, I wake up to the gentle noise of its surf, cooling sea winds, and pleasant odors. Every day, I walk its beaches and watch the pure white clouds build. I play in its afternoon showers like a child. I lounge in its lagoon, enjoy meals of my own choosing, provide my own companionship, explore the past with my books and relax after dinner with my bourbon and memories of Mary Margaret. Oftentimes, I just sit on the beach and watch the sand crabs feed.

And every evening, there is a Polynesian sunset.

EPILOGUE

Excerpted from *The FIJI TIMES*

Suva November 12, 2001. Donald Foster, owner and sole resident of Vaka Malua Island, thirty miles southeast of Suva, was found dead last evening by Charles Dobson, manager of the Fiji Hilton, and the hotel helicopter pilot, Ian Flannary. The body was discovered on the north beach of Vaka Malua from the air as the Hilton people were preparing to land for a routine visit with Mister Foster.

The remains were dressed in an American World War Two Marine Corps service dress green uniform and half-seated in a cramped bamboo cage on the north beach near the western volcanic rim segment. According to the Hilton pilot, Mister Foster appeared to have been deceased only a day or so. Beside him were a green metal box of documents, shell remnants from a recently eaten mangrove crab and a three-quarters empty bottle of Early Times bourbon whiskey.

Preliminary findings by the municipal

coroner indicate that Mister Foster died of natural causes. There was no evidence of foul play. No explanation has been offered as to why the body was in the cage.

When contacted at the Fiji Hilton, hotel manager Dobson stated, "Mister Foster was a good friend and this is completely unexpected. At our last meeting on Vaka Malua, he was depressed over the recent increase in racial violence, social strife and government instability of his native land. Besides that, the April loss of his adopted family, Niko and Sarah Timaru along with their two-year-old daughter, Mary Margaret, in a sailing accident south of Oahu, quite possibly had a devastating effect on his state of mind."

General Sitiveni Rabuka, retired prime minister and a close friend of Foster, issued the following statement through a spokesman, "The Republic of Fiji has lost a valued citizen and I have lost a treasured friend. Donald Foster was a proud American and a responsible white Fijian who had the utmost respect for our people and culture. He honored us by his residence."

According to Detective Tom Mara of the Suva Police Department who is conducting a routine investigation of the death, Mister Foster left a last will and testament which specifies that his remains be buried on Vaka Malua in the bamboo grove on the eastern tip of the island. The will also directs that all man-made improvements on the island are to be removed and the single passage through the surrounding reef be permanently blocked.

Mister Foster apparently had no heirs and his will further provides for the ownership of Vaka Malua to be returned to the Republic of Fiji as long as it is kept as his burial island. The balance of his estate will go to the Polynesian Cultural Center on the north shore of the Hawaiian Island of Oahu.

(end copy)

ABOUT THE AUTHOR

Born in Memphis, Tennessee, M.E. Morris lives with his wife Virginia in Colorado Springs, near their nine children and their families. He is a retired Navy Captain. He started writing professionally in 1986 after a thirty-year career as a Naval Aviator. The Sand Crabs is his seventh novel.

His writing awards include a National Freedom Foundation Honor Award, and two Top Hand Awards from the Colorado Authors League. He is a regular faculty member at the Pike's Peak Writers Conference, and a long-time member of the Published Authors League of the Rocky Mountain Fiction Writers.

Mr. Morris holds a BS degree in Nautical Science, an MS degree in International Relations, and is a graduate of the Senior Course of the Naval War College. He is also a member of the Navy League of the United States, The Daedalians (Order of Military Pilots), and the Association of Naval Aviation.

His hobbies include aviation and photography. He built and flew his own Experimental Class aircraft, and his photographic work has been professionally published.

He has traveled extensively in Polynesia and Micronesia, and holds an abiding passion for the peoples of the Pacific Triangle; he is an avid student of their economic potential, and their political progress.